# OTHER WORKS
## by BENJAMIN WALLACE

### *NOVELS*

Post-Apocalyptic Nomadic Warriors:
A Duck & Cover Adventure

Tortugas Rising

### *DUMB WHITE HUSBAND*

The Big Book of Dumb White Husband

### *GUIDES*

The Dumb White Husband's Guide to Babies

Giving The Bird: The Indie Author's Guide to Twitter

*Visit benjaminwallacebooks.com for more info.*

BY

BENJAMIN WALLACE

*For Sam, Sam, Brandon, Chris, Jess, Matt, James*
*and everyone else who helped create the Stockwell mythos*
*when we were just stupid kids.*

# PRELUDE

He collapsed. Partially from exhaustion, mostly from the native-hewn dart in his leg. The jungle floor welcomed him with the smell of rotted vegetation and the dampness of a billion drops of rain. It struck him hard.

His panic overcame his shortness of breath and he turned on to his back and stared up at the seemingly impenetrable jungle wall. How he had run so far was beyond him.

There was sound and no sound. A maddening silence that reverberated in his mind as his widened eyes struggled to see through the vines and trees. The pounding may have been coming from his chest. He had run for what seemed hours and his heart crashed at his rib cage to be let free, to abandon the body and continue running, but his leg said no.

He risked a glance from the darkness to his leg. The barb had fallen free, but it still hurt. The pain was unjustly disproportionate to the wound. Had the barb been poisonous? Even now, as the blood rushed through his veins, was a primitive toxin nearing closer to his heart?

A crack; it was unlike them. They had moved silently upon him in the growth of darkness. He had heard nothing until the whistling of the blowgun. It was only then, once he had been struck, that they appeared—dozens of them, stepping as if from the shadows to surround him. Each warrior dressed only in a sparse bit of cloth about his waist and a hideous mask before his face. They moved like the dead, silent and wraithlike, as they closed the circle about him.

Had it not been for the now useless rifle he carried, he would have fallen earlier. Blazing round after round into the throng of natives, he had cleaved a path to freedom and let the jungle envelop him.

Now they emerged, the jungle's darkness providing no hindrance in their pursuit. One by one the demon faces of the masks appeared around him, staring with sightless eyes into the opening where he had fallen.

He summoned his will to live and stood on his near useless limb. Grasping his rifle by the barrel, he screamed, though the masks had no ears, "Come, you godless heathens! I'll shatter each one of your ugly faces!"

Not one of the masks moved or even blinked. There was only silence in response. Then a whistle shattered the still. He grabbed his leg and fell to the foreign soil. His breathing slowed. His taunts were a weak spill from his throat.

Weak, like an infant trying to lift a rattle that some cruel uncle had filled with lead, he pulled his right arm across his chest and lifted his head.

"Dam. Dam." The words drifted past his teeth as he lost control of his lips.

He couldn't move. The paralysis took from him the will to resist. From the jungle emerged a dark shadow. What dim light broke through the growth revealed an object in the shadow's hand. The shadow moved closer and held forth the object; a carved death mask, chiseled from nightmares. The shadow placed the mask upon the fallen man's face.

Through these horrible eyes he saw bright flashes of light, a prism of pain. Then all became dark. All was quiet. He saw nothing. He heard nothing. He felt nothing. Yet he moved.

# 1

## The Giant Awakens

Damian Stockwell, captain-of-industry, PhD, man-of-action, awoke entwined in frilly, pink sheets. Lace curtains hung from the bed's canopy and filtered the early morning light into a soft glow as it began to break through the window.

Years had passed since he had experienced any transition between asleep and alert. Through dedicated practice and sheer force of will, he had trained himself to be fully aware of his surroundings the moment his eyes opened. The ability had saved his life countless times. Cowards were not uncommon in the world and they would sooner strike the helpless than confront a conscious man.

There was no danger here. He lay in the comfort of a luxurious bed next to a gorgeous woman. He looked to the lady sleeping next to him. Blonde hair covered her features, but he knew them well. Beneath the golden locks were the delicate cheekbones and fine skin of a woman that lived amid the parties and pleasantries of high society. Behind the closed lids were the rich brown eyes of the woman he loved.

Beautiful and peaceful, she slept; her chest rose and fell with even breaths that signaled a restful slumber. Her tranquility stirred in him a thought to wake her; together they could relive the passion of the night before.

There were two ways to subtly awaken and arouse a woman that did not require a beachfront setting or diamond jewelry. The first involved the pollen of an exotic flower that grew only on a peak in Tristan da Cunha. Properly harvested, the flower's scent excited the more delicate portions of the female mind and released a flood of hormones and desires into her body. Through thorough laboratory testing, he had learned that the effect was almost identical in nature to when a woman sees a man cooking in an apron. He did not have this flower or an apron.

The second method, however, required no flora or cooking utensils. It required nothing but a precise and gentle touch. He had learned of it years ago in the ancient city of Timbuktu. The city had been the final destination in an automobile race that had taken him across the sands of the Sahara. Crossing the finish line had led him not only to victory in the Timbuktu in '32 rally, but also to the city's legendary library.

Timbuktu's rich legacy as a trading hub had brought more than spices to its walls. The trading of books had led to its development as a center of knowledge unlike any other in the ancient world. East met west and ideas were traded freely. Books, parchments and scrolls recorded this exchange of thought. This lore was stored in the library and protected throughout the centuries.

In a dusty corner of the mud walled building, somehow dustier than the others, he had found an ancient Mali script that shared the secrets of the forbidden arts. Casting glances over his shoulder, he had unrolled the scroll and scanned it quickly, committing the ancient text to memory in both its native language and English. He did not want to risk a mistranslation. Considering the delicacy of the subject matter, he feared that an error in his linguist's tongue could result in injury. Someone could lose an eye or, at the very least, a great deal of dignity.

Many of the sordid details in the scroll were an affront to his gentlemanly character. He led a forthright life of decency and much of what he read in the vulgar scroll challenged what he believed to be morally right. Yet his scientist's mind had compelled him to read the text in full as his thirst for knowledge was insatiable and an understanding of other cultures, even their depravity, could one day mean the difference between life and death. So, he read each passage carefully, skipping none but those that made reference to "engorged like a water laden camel."

Now, back in New York, the lace curtains turned yellow sunlight into rays of pink that fell upon his lover's face. He recalled a singular passage from the scroll and moved his right arm across the rising chest of Dahlia Singleton. His fingers found the ninth rib on her left side—the side closest to her heart.

Proper pressure and rhythm applied between the ninth and tenth ribs would wake any woman in a state of desire. The wrong rhythm, the wrong pressure or the wrong location, and the object of one's desire would awake in a fit of giggling.

Damian had found the proper cadence hidden within the passage itself. The verse, if read in Mali, relayed to the observant reader the proper measure that brought passion. He repeated it to himself once in the native tongue and placed his finger on her rib.

He tapped. An alarm sounded. Dahlia giggled and slapped him across the face, never waking from her slumber.

Stockwell looked to his wristwatch. The alarm continued and the face of the dial began to flash red. It was not loud, but this quiet warble had stolen his attention from the sleeping beauty before him and disrupted his rhythm. The watch face flashed twice more before it became a pulsing crimson. It throbbed slowly like the final heartbeats of a dying man.

His fears had been confirmed; he did not begrudge his lapse in attention. Damian Stockwell slid from the pink, frilly sheets and moved quickly about the room, gathering his clothes. A black tuxedo jacket was hung neatly across the back of a chair; the rest of his attire was scattered about the room and he set about collecting the pieces. As he retrieved his outerwear, he turned each article inside out, converting the formal wear to a worker's uniform. The navy blue cotton was wash-worn and sooty in places.

Dahlia stirred. Her manicured hands reached out for him and felt the empty space next to her in the bed. She awoke within a haze of sleep. Sitting up, she saw Damian dressed in the costume and fell back into bed searching for a pillow. "Dam. No more games. Not now."

"I'm afraid this is no game, my darling. I'm needed and I'll not risk tarnishing your reputation by having anyone see me leave here."

She found the satin pillow and drew it across her face. "Okay."

"I regret that I must leave at all."

"It's okay," her voice drifted away.

"I wish I could stay, but it's a matter of life or death."

"It's fine, really." She tried to roll away and back to sleep.

He stepped silently up to her and pulled the pillow from her face. Her skin was radiant. Even half asleep she was full of life. He leaned in and kissed her deeply. He felt her tiredness evaporate as she reached up and embraced him. Her kiss was full of a passion that no ancient Mali trickery could conjure.

Lifting her from the bed into his arms took little effort. He matched the passion in her lips. Regretfully, he concluded the kiss and set her back into the bed.

She looked at him and sighed, "Oh, Dam. You're all man."

"I know. Can I borrow your mascara?"

Costume alone is not a disguise. The mere application of accessories and makeup serve only to cover a man, not transform him into another. The simple application of cloth and cosmetic could be learned by any novice in a theater group, but for a disguise to pass beyond the lights of the great white way, it took an artist dedicated to the craft of subterfuge.

Given the proper time, Damian Stockwell could transform his thick six-foot-four frame into that of an elderly matron, hunched at the shoulders and suffering from the gout. But, the intensity of the light on his wristwatch indicated that he did not have such time.

Rubbed briskly between his fingers, Dahlia's mascara had provided the right amount of coal dust he required. Separated from the petroleum jelly and applied to his face, the dust matched the soot upon his clothes and brought unity to the physical aspects of his disguise.

It didn't take much. A single unsightly blemish, he knew, would contrast from his striking features and draw attention from his presence. One distraction was all it took. Under interrogation, he doubted that even the most observant fellow would be able to identify the color of Stockwell's eyes—striking silver-blue.

As he rode down in the elevator car, he donned the rest of the disguise. It went far beyond appearance. It went beyond the physical and into his very being. Stockwell did not merely dress in a dirty blue shirt with the name Tom embroidered across the chest; he became Tom.

Damian's shoulders sank; Tom was meek. Too timid to ask for a raise, the man lived in squalor with his wife, three beautiful children and two ugly ones. Damian frowned; Tom loved his children, but by working two shifts to pay for rent, food, and makeup for the ugly children, he never had time to see them. Guilt measured against obligation but he was powerless to change the situation for Tom was an honorable man and he had to provide for his family first and address his own needs second.

A mechanical chime sounded and the elevator operator announced that they had reached the ground floor. The doors opened and he stepped into a bustling lobby.

Damian smiled through Tom's frown. He was delighted to see the mass of people. He had always believed that the more people there were around, the easier it was to go unseen. Being another face in the crowd, while difficult for Damian, was something to which Tom had grown accustomed.

His footsteps were absorbed by the plush carpet. This was fortunate as Damian limped; Tom had a bad leg. Tom told people that the affliction was the result of an old war wound but, in truth, the limp came from a near fatal foxtrot misstep in the '20s.

Damian crossed the room, excusing himself as he went; Tom was polite, if not confident. His apologies were mumbled and spoken with his head down. Still, no one noticed him. As always, Damian had chosen a disguise appropriate for the setting. The wealthy and well-reared patrons that filled the lobby were trained to ignore someone dressed as a plumber. Should Tom try to make eye contact, they would avert their gaze. Should he try to converse with them, they would signal for security. Not fitting in was the perfect way to disappear.

Damian stopped to pick a piece of trash from the floor; Tom was fastidious. It wasn't that Tom abhorred litter, but he had once received a reprimand for ignoring a gum wrapper that had been dropped on the floor and he feared a repeat of the incident. He could not afford to jeopardize his job. Should he find himself in the breadline, Jenny would undoubtedly leave him. Damian shed a tear; Tom wept. Tom loved his wife dearly and wished he could provide her with a better life. He had failed her as a provider. Of course, she wouldn't see it that way. She still loved him after all of these years. He was the father of both her beautiful and ugly children and he would always be the man of her dreams.

Dropping the litter in the trashcan, Damian exited through the revolving door; Tom struggled against the weight. He put his shoulder into the door and grunted as he shoved. Tom worried that he was getting weaker. He had always been able-bodied and strong, but lately he feared he had contracted something that was sapping his strength. It made him panic to think that it was anything serious—the fear of leaving Jenny and the kids behind was too much. Shrugging his shoulders, he self-diagnosed the ever-growing weakness as a cold and pushed through to the other side of the revolving door.

The air was bitterly cold, but the warmth of the doorman's smile was genuine and Tom matched it.

"Good day." Tom's voice was gruff, shredded and raspy. He lit a cigarette and drew deeply the fine tobacco. Damian never smoked, but all of his disguises did.

Murray MacDonald stood proud in his uniform. Brass buttons blazed in the rays of what early morning sun managed to break through the buildings of New York. Golden braids adorned the shoulders of the wool jacket that he had buttoned high to keep out the winter cold. The sentry was old but still capable of ushering on the hobos and unwashed masses from under the building's canopy.

"Good morning, Mr. Stockwell. I sent Henry for your driver."

"Beg your pardon, sir. The name's Tom."

"I'm sorry, Mr. Stockwell?"

Damian drew deep on the Camel hoping to aid the raspy voice. "Not Stockwell. Tom. I'm the plumber; there was a problem on fourteen. A plumbing problem. They called me in to clear things up."

The doorman appeared puzzled.

"Which I did. Because I'm the plumber."

One long look and the doorman laughed. "Oh, you really had me going, Mr. Stockwell."

"Dammit, MacTavish. How did you know it was me?"

"I'm sorry, sir?"

"The disguise. How do you do it? And every time? This particular disguise has fooled master criminals, newsmen, and even my own mother."

Murray appeared shaken. "My apologies, sir. Perhaps you just have a certain aura about you."

"No. That can't be it. My aura is also disguised as a plumber."

"A lucky guess then, sir?"

Damian Stockwell put his hand on the old Scot's shoulder and smiled. "I don't think so, my friend. Luck favors the weak-minded. And you are not weak-minded."

The doorman smiled and stood a little taller.

"So, it's not luck then. It must be that leprechaun magic. Isn't it?"

Murray MacDonald shrunk inside his jacket. "Sir, that's Iri...Yes, sir. That must be it."

Stockwell chuckled deep and rich. "Of course it is. Now be a good chap and forget you saw me here this morning." Stockwell shook the doorman's hand and deposited a large bill in his white glove.

"Of course, sir."

A black and silver Duesenberg pulled up in front of the building. Its vast stretches of chrome stole the gleam from the doorman's brass as it rolled through the rays of light. The valet, tall and broad-chested, stepped out of the limo and walked around the vehicle to open the door for his charge.

Stockwell slapped the doorman on the back. "Thank you for your discretion, MacTavish." He then turned his attention to the valet. "You can relax, Bertrand. It's me."

The valet nodded and Stockwell stepped into the car.

Once inside, Tom was forgotten. The problems with the man's family and his ugly children were his own. Like the seamless transition of dawn, he shed the persona of the miserable plumber and became Damian Stockwell—doer of good.

The valet slid into the driver's seat of the luxurious limousine.

"That doorman is a good man, Bertrand."

The Frenchman peered into the rearview mirror. "Oui, Monsieur. MacDonald is a good man. "

"No detail escapes his eye. A very observant fellow, that MacTavish. Almost as observant as myself."

Outside the car, Murray MacDonald gave Stockwell a white-gloved finger. Stockwell continued, "I feel better knowing Dahlia is under his watchful eye."

Bertrand checked his blind spot. "Oui, Monsieur. What is our destination this fine morning?"

Damian stared at the pulsing dial of his wristwatch. The intensity had not faded. "Home, Bertrand." Stockwell held up his watch so the valet could see the glowing face. "Our help is needed."

"Oui, Monsieur." Bertrand pulled away from the curb and maneuvered gracefully into the morning traffic. If called upon he could unleash the full power of the limo's retooled engine and overtake any target or lose any tail. Few drivers in the world could match the Frenchman's skill behind the wheel. He could play the powerful and silent engine with the skill of a musician.

As the car glided through the early morning Manhattan traffic, Damian Stockwell removed the physical elements of his plumber's disguise and pondered the glowing watch. The dial was designed to communicate a vast array of signals using various colors. Blue indicated that all was well. This calming hue was used in the field when verbal signals or thumbs up were rendered ineffective due to distance or darkness. Yellow meant caution. Like a traffic light or the flash of evil in a cat's eyes, this color was meant to warn of a possible danger. Green meant dinner.

But red—red was the color of pain and signified that someone was in grave peril. The dial's only shortcoming was that it could not identify a point of origin. Damian had compatriots around the globe and each was entrusted with an identical communicator. Remarkably, the signal could have come from anywhere in the world.

He glanced frequently at the watch, hoping it would transition to blue. But, the crimson dial did not change. Whoever had called him was still in peril. There was no use in speculating which of his associates had sent the distress call. Questions would be answered when they reached his office. Though the device itself was ignorant to the sender's location, the distress signal also broadcast a coded radio transmission. This information would be sent by relay stations around the world to his office where it would be decoded.

He would know soon enough who had requested his help and to where he should rush to their aid.

Wiping the soot from his chin removed this final element of the disguise and restored more than Damian's dashing good looks. It enabled his personality to become dominant again and he could dedicate his full faculties to the problem at hand. Evil beware.

# 2

## A Stranger in the Shadows

He watched from across the street. Hidden in the shadow of an oak tree and concealed by a staircase, he watched from beneath the brim of his hat as the Duesenberg arrived at the five-story brownstone. The glint from the chrome had arrived moments before the car, warning him of its presence. He retreated further into the shadows.

The sight of his prey surprised him. The man's stature had not been misrepresented. He had thought for certain that the profile had been an exaggeration. The language they had used to describe the target had sounded like hyperbole. Who could truly be that big? The dossier's contents had described a man that was larger than life itself. He had questioned the description: thick like the trunk of a tree, arms like coiled pythons, a chest the breadth of a man's reach. Impossible. Seeing him now, however, it was clear that the report did little justice to the titan that emerged from the vehicle.

He was tremendous. Well over six feet in a world of much shorter men. The distance between his shoulders could not be much less. As the blonde-haired giant strode to his doorway, passersby were pulled from their own focus. Couples stopped talking. Newspapers were ignored. It was as if this man's mere presence had created a gravity that attracted attention.

He watched Stockwell smile and greet several of the pedestrians before moving to the entrance of the brownstone. There the giant stopped and turned to survey the street.

He ducked behind the stairwell. Did he see him? He couldn't have. The staircase hid him. Concealment gave him courage and he inched closer to the edge of the stairs to look back across the street.

Stockwell's glance landed on nothing. It merely passed over the street. He continued to smile and greet those on the sidewalk.

This gave the man comfort but, still, the giant's glance was terrifying. There was no malice in the steel gray eyes—far from it. Perhaps it was this fact that made the base of his neck tingle as if it had been lit upon by a spider. He knew the man was scanning the street, noting changes, discrepancies, and the people strolling by. But, it had been so casual, so natural that it had caused him pause.

He felt the package under his arm and unconsciously stroked the brown paper wrapping. This brought him comfort and he felt some relief. His plan was not without risk, but if the man in the house suspected nothing, then the only time he would have to lay eyes on Damian Stockwell again was to confirm the kill.

The Duesenberg pulled away from the home. The valet had departed, as was routine, to park the car. Stockwell disappeared through the front door.

He waited for a few moments, keeping a careful eye on the door and windows of the five-story home. There were no eyes in the windows. Since Stockwell had entered, foot traffic on the sidewalk had resumed its normal pattern. After several moments, he was confident that the street was not being watched.

Stepping from behind the staircase, he held the package tighter under his arm. Nondescript brown paper was sealed in twine. The sender's address was a clever forgery. The recipient was labeled as the house across the street.

Looking both ways, he stepped onto the residential street and crossed quickly to the door of the brownstone. He set the package down and prayed that the plan would work. After seeing the man, the idea of having to kill Stockwell on his own frightened him.

He rushed back across the street to the safety of the stairs and had just settled into his shelter of shadows as the valet returned.

His attention had not been on Stockwell's companion. The driver was almost the size of Stockwell himself. Not as broad, but tall and thick, the valet would prove a formidable opponent for anyone.

The man in the shadows smiled. The plan would work.

The valet walked up to the front door, picked up the package, and entered the sanctuary of Damian Stockwell.

Bertrand studied the package in his hands. Had his employer not seen it on the stoop? It was unlike him to miss something. Bertrand shrugged; the distress call would have his employer's full attention.

The Frenchman read the address; it was from a movie studio in California. This explained it being left on the stoop. Damian held little fascination with motion pictures, but the feeling was not mutual. Though he had made it clear that he would never allow his name or likeness to be used for a feature picture, the studios persisted. Stockwell's adventures were the perfect fare for exciting films. As such, the studios were always trying to woo him. Gifts and pleas arrived often. It was not unusual that these offerings were delivered in the arms of the studio's latest starlet. But, Stockwell wouldn't yield. He would send the starlets back in the morning with the gift in hand and a "thank you but no thank you" note.

It was no wonder that the silver screen wanted his blessings. Stockwell's adventures were epic in scope, harrowing in tone, and always morally sound. It was for exactly this reason that the man declined both movie deals and interviews. A life such as his was not for the meek or feeble. Fearing for their safety, he did not want to expose impressionable youth to such excitement. To see his exploits glorified would put ideas into their young minds. Ideas would become dreams and dreams would become mistakes.

Whenever a proposal arrived, the result was the same. Stockwell would dictate a note claiming that he was flattered but found no interest in their "make believe fantasies" and the gift would be returned.

This package would be no different. It would be opened, commented on, and sent back with no blessings given.

Bertrand tucked the package under his arm and moved through the halls to the radio room. There he found Damian adjusting the dials on a large cabinet. It stood seven feet tall and its surface was covered with switches and knobs. In the center of the machine was a circular glass screen. The screen itself was only a small part of the device but it was this that commanded Damian's focus.

A warm hum emanated from the rich wood casing. A series of squelches and squeals joined in the chorus of technological tones as Damian adjusted the controls.

Bertrand addressed his employer, "Have you located the problem, Monsieur?"

"Not yet, Bertrand. It still takes some fine-tuning. Hopefully Philo will have the kinks worked out in the next version."

Bertrand nodded. Philo T. Farnsworth was a brilliant young mind that Stockwell had encountered at the Franklin Institute in Philadelphia a few short years before. Farnsworth's presentation on something he had called television was met with skepticism from the audience. Damian Stockwell, however, had always put a great deal of faith in science. He knew that a powerful imagination mixed with sound reason had the power to change the world.

Damian had seen beyond Philo's vision and contracted the inventor to develop Stockwell's worldwide transmission network. They had called it DamVision; DV for short.

Once the distress signal in the watch had been activated, a camera and a microphone began to transmit sound and images across the private radio network that Stockwell had secretly installed around the globe. Every signal was directed to the DV where Damian could decode the message and react accordingly. Bertrand still marveled at the brilliance of it all.

"What have you got there, Bertrand?" Stockwell had not looked up from the dials but had somehow noticed the package under the valet's arm.

"A package, Monsieur. It was on the stoop."

"Hmmm. I didn't see it when I came in. Who's it from?"

"Hollywood, Monsieur."

"Ha, those folks can't get enough of my tales. But, still, they never learn. Well," Stockwell stepped away from the monitor, "open it up and let's see what their latest attempt to win my approval looks like."

Bertrand smiled and set the package down. He pulled a penknife from his pocket and cut the twine. His excitement built as he tore away the paper.

"Careful, Bertrand. It's not Christmas. We'll want to reuse that paper."

"Of course, Monsieur." His excitement had gotten the better of him. The packages often contained autographs from Hollywood's biggest stars, props from famous movies, and even personal pleas and pledges of love from the town's leading ladies. Despite his employer's lack of enthusiasm for the silver screen, Bertrand was an ardent fan. He spent his free evenings in the center row of the cinema soaking in the flickering light of the world's greatest storytellers.

He opened the box inside the package. He jumped. A horrific tiki mask stared back at him. Carved with jagged edges into the wood, the sneer alone gave the brave Frenchman pause. He felt violated by its gaze. Eyes like black-glass stared into his soul. He was hesitant to pick it up.

"Hmm. There's no note. I guess we can't return this one." Stockwell pulled the mask from the box. "It's a ghastly thing. They must be trying to do a story about one of my South American adventures."

"Perhaps you will reconsider this time, Monsieur?"

"Ha," Damian slapped his friend and fellow adventurer on the back. "That's my Frenchman. Lured by the thin veneer of the cinema. I know you're a fan of these moving pictures, my friend, but I feel I have a responsibility to the world. I can't have my exploits exploited. Impressionable children would be in the audience and I will not be responsible for their attempts to mimic me. You've been with me for years, Bertrand. You know how dangerous my life is. My anecdotes alone could injure thousands."

"Oui, Monsieur."

"You know better than anyone the degree to which I prepare myself to combat villainy. I train vigorously to outfight the forces of evil and study vigorouslier to outsmart them. If anyone went up against them without proper training or education … the results would be disastrous."

"Of course. You are right, Monsieur."

"Of course I am."

"Still, to one day see Hollywood, that would be something, non?"

"Of course, my friend. And I have no doubt that one day our paths will lead us there. But, in the meantime, we have work to do." Stockwell dropped the mask back into the box, smiled at his friend and returned to the DamVision monitor.

"It's coming in now, Bertrand. We'll have answers in a moment."

Bertrand stared at the mask. Transfixed by its horrid features, his face began to mimic the fearful expression carved into the wood.

"Come, you godless heathens! I'll shatter each one of your ugly faces!" The voice from the DV was clear. The panic played in the radio room as if the victim sat with them. The fact that it could have been transmitted from another hemisphere was another remarkable achievement for the man they called the Man of Marvels.

Damian recognized the voice that echoed through the room. "It's Simmons, Bertrand. Simmons is in danger."

Bertrand had heard the audio play, but he was not listening. He reached for the mask and felt the grain of the cold, dead wood. Grooves cut deep in the surface created shadows within even the smoothest areas. It was indeed horrific but somehow irresistible.

"Dam! Dam!" The voice on the DamVision pleaded for help as the image finally began to appear. It was fuzzy at first. Stockwell's fingers flew between knobs and switches and with each twist and tweak, the picture became clearer.

"Sinister cowards," Damian swore at the screen as the scene in the jungle unfolded.

Bertrand pulled the mask from the box and held it before his face.

The adjustment Stockwell made to the dial was imperceptible, but it brought into focus the final view of Peter Simmons. "Oh, my ..." Damian uttered and turned towards his valet. "Don't put on that mask!"

But, it was too late. Bertrand set his face inside the mask. Through the soulless black eyes he saw bright flashes of light, a prism of pain. Then all became dark. All was quiet. He saw nothing. He heard nothing. He felt nothing. Yet he moved.

# 3

## Through the Mask Darkly

Though still in an experimental stage, the DamVision monitor had revealed the final sight that Peter Simmons's eyes had beheld. A hand had extended and forced upon the wounded man a horrific mask with soulless eyes. The chiseled expression upon its face was one of agony—a man screaming, not in pain, but from the consciousness of a growing and unstoppable madness.

Black and white images quivered with atmospheric interference, the machine's weak link was not the technology but the earth itself. Well-defined shapes blurred as the mask passed over the lens of the communicator that was strapped to Simmons's wrist. The image was lost completely for a moment but reappeared as the villain's hand, now free of the mask, retreated from view.

There was only the night sky. The small lens in the watch registered the stars beyond the thick canopy of the jungle. The only movement was the swaying of the branches before the stars.

Stockwell envisioned the thickness in the jungle air as he waited
for the camera in the wristwatch to give some other clue to his
friend's final location. He was all too familiar with the oppressive
humidity of the world's jungles. His photographic memory went
beyond images and sounds. His skin crawled with the sweat that a
jungle produced. This seeping sensation was dotted with the
memory of the myriad of bugs that would land on his skin. He
brushed at his arms as he peered into the monitor.

The world was full of wonders. Beauty could be found even
in the driest desert, the deepest caves, or Detroit. But, jungles were
his least favorite of the world's environments. It wasn't the danger
present in the creatures, the plants or the rivers. It wasn't that
everything seemed to exist just to kill a man. It was the ick.

His vow to thwart evil, however, took him to jungles more
often than not. Hiding from the eyes of the world was easy in the
tangle of vines and webs. Villains often chose to hide deep in these
dark places that dripped and crawled with yuck.

The shift in the camera was sudden. At first, Damian
assumed one of the attackers had seized the device from
Simmons's wrist. Each was constructed of gold for both functional
and boasting purposes and would fetch a grand price in any corner
of the world. Moments later it became clear that the device was
still strapped to his compatriot. The camera movements were
smooth as Simmons somehow found the strength to rise to his feet.

Stockwell watched his friend pull the barbs from his leg. It
had no doubt been a poison on their tips that had brought him
down. But, any poison capable of falling his friend could not have
worn off so quickly. The man would be lucky if such a toxin did
not stop his heart. Despite his deduction, Simmons began to rise.
As the weakened man stood, the perspective of the watch gave
Damian one last glance at the pursuers.

For a brief moment, beyond the focal point in a dark blur,
Stockwell could see the outline of several men. Each wore a
horrific mask identical to the one thrust at Simmons. Then the
watch turned as Simmons peered into the dial. Staring back was

the horrific visage that Bertrand now held in his hands. Simmons disabled the watch.

Damian had tried to shout to his valet, but his warning came too late. Bertrand stood silently before him, staring through the dead glass of the mask's eyes. The shark-like lenses permitted no light to pass and he could not see the eyes of his trusted friend and servant.

"Bertrand?"

The Frenchman was still. His hands had fallen to his sides. His body had gone rigid. He stood like a plank in the center of the radio room. He made no move to acknowledge Damian. It was as if the Frenchman simply wasn't there.

"Bertrand!" Even as he rushed to his friend, Stockwell's incredible mind raced through a thousand explanations for the man's sudden inactivity. There were chemicals and gases that would have such an effect but the mask had not been in place long enough.

Simmons had succumbed quickly to the mask's control and Damian was certain that Bertrand would undoubtedly suffer the same fate if the demon's face was not removed. Stockwell dashed across the room with blazing speed.

The kick to his face was faster.

Bertrand's right leg caught Damian under the chin and snapped his head back. The strike forced him back into a shelf of radio equipment. The devices he and his team used to communicate scattered across the floor as the shelf collapsed.

Stockwell straightened and looked to his friend. Bertrand seemed unmoved by the attack. He stood rigid in the center of the room.

Damian rubbed his square jaw and focused on the problem at hand. "Bertrand. You've got an ugly look about you that I will now slap from your face."

The mask stared back in silent mockery.

"How dare you say nothing."

Stockwell launched at his friend.

The rigid posture vanished. Bertrand fell into a defensive stance that Damian knew all too well. Inside the massive man, there was a shudder. He stopped cold.

Bertrand possessed a control over his emotions like no man Stockwell had ever met. It was that professional demeanor that made him the perfect valet. But, under the calm exterior lurked the dangerous spirit of a vicious savateur.

The pair had first met in combat and Stockwell had seen first-hand Bertrand's savate skills employed to devastating effect. He had developed an immediate respect for the man. It's true that many friendships begin this way, but Bertrand and Damian had been on opposing sides.

Stockwell had fought on the side of good. Bertrand was under contract to a Parisian crime lord known only as La Grenouille. The two titans had collided and fought to exhaustion.

Though slightly smaller in stature than Stockwell, the Frenchman had delivered a punishing assault using a combination of savate and judo. Damian had been forced to use a variety of combat systems to find openings in the Frenchman's fury.

The fight had continued for an hour, spilling from the crime lord's hideout and into the streets of Paris. Not since Napoleon had trod with tiny strides had the cobblestones of the city been witness to such great warriors. Stockwell exhausted his extensive knowledge of martial arts, boxing and throwing things during the encounter. Had it not been for a well-placed portrait artist, Stockwell could not even honestly say that he would have defeated the Frenchman.

The altercation had ended with a total of three broken bones, one angry French portrait artist and the hiring of Bertrand as his personal valet. He had employed the man out of respect, but also as insurance that he would never have to face Bertrand's savagery again.

But, now his friend stood before him, ready to unleash his brutal fighting skills.

Stockwell calculated his chances. He knew that it had to be the mask that had caused his friend to strike. Therefore, his attacks would focus on removing the mask. If this could be done quickly, they may avoid endangering the good people and portrait artists of New York.

Damian dropped into his own defensive stance. His technique was of his own creation. On his many adventures around the world, he had studied with the great masters of several exotic martial arts. Over the years he had selected the finest techniques and incorporated them into his own martial art—Damitsu.

Proven in countless fights, he had never doubted the system. But, now he knew it would take all of his skill and strength to defeat his friend without killing him. It would not be easy or painless. For the first time that he could remember, he did not envy himself.

Bertrand burst forward. Knees and feet blurred as he quickly closed the distance between them.

Stockwell was on the defensive. Every hand and foot he had was employed in blocking Bertrand's strikes. Bruises formed quickly on his forearms and shins as they collided with Bertrand's relentless offense.

The Frenchman was fast. Faster, even, than Stockwell remembered. Lefts and rights, fists and feet, blended together in the air before him. Damian was forced around the room as the valet tirelessly launched blow after blow. He could do nothing but leave his motions to his reflexes.

Cursing, he reeled back. It had taken the promise of a large salary and the death of an underworld chief to attain Bertrand's service—all with the intent of never having to fight the man again. Now, even the threat of terminating his employment would not be enough to stop the vicious valet.

Damian was driven back into the DV cabinet. The jar set the device to replay. Simmons's voice pleaded over the speakers, "Dam. Dam."

The great adventurer dove to the right as Bertrand struck. The fist missed him by inches and continued through the vacuum tube of the DamVision set. Sparks flew. Blood flowed. But, Bertrand continued his attack—unfazed by the shard of glass now protruding from between his knuckles.

The glass grazed Stockwell's cheek and drew blood. His lethal friend had become even more deadly. He could no longer wait to unleash his own offense. He rolled behind the DV cabinet and brought the apparatus crashing down between the two of them.

The obstacle gave him the fraction of a second he needed to change the tide of the fight. Employing a combination of boxing and elements from the Canadian Combato defense system, he stepped forward with a series of jabs and crosses. The techniques had proven unstoppable in previous encounters; Bertrand, however, exposed several flaws in the system as his powerful strikes and kicks continued to slip through Stockwell's offense.

His own blows landed with little effect. He felt muscle yield as he struck. He knew that he was connecting with full force, but there was no response, no cries of pain, no "ughs" of agony, from the valet. Blows such as these had knocked out cattle, but the Frenchman kept coming.

Damian was knocked back against the radio room's door. Bertrand struck again with a straight right. Damian caught the fist but it drove with the force of a cinderblock thrown by a gorilla holding a grudge. The shard of glass from the monitor dug deep into Stockwell's hand. Ignoring the pain, he grunted as the power of the strike drove his own hands into his chest and his body through the door.

The solid core splintered as he crashed into the fifth floor hallway. He rolled to his feet in time to deflect a left foot and absorb a right in his ribs. He felt nothing break. His ribs had held, but he made a general observation that most of him was starting to feel squishy.

A quick onslaught of knees backed him to the head of the stairway. He slipped over the banister and began to descend. He needed distance. His initial fear had been defeating Bertrand without injuring his friend; now he was struggling to remain on his feet.

The Frenchman seemed unstoppable. The mask that had robbed him of his humanity seemed to increase the speed of his movements and the power behind each strike. Punching through the glass tube of the DV had also proven that his nerves were no longer in control. Bertrand was tough, but no man, not even Stockwell, was immune to pain such as that.

Bertrand continued to punch without hesitation despite the glass shard impaled between his knuckles. It was as if the foreign object did not even register.

The Frenchman leapt over the railing and landed in front of Damian midway down the flight. The raving mask stared up at Stockwell. He became enraged at the inanimate face that had taken his friend from him, but he did not scream, he did not swear. He dove.

Colliding headfirst into the valet's chest, the two crashed and rolled down the stairs. For a brief moment, Stockwell found his hand on the mask. He pulled at its edge and he felt the mask begin to give.

An elbow crashed into his solar plexus. The breath was forced from his lungs as the point of the elbow began to grind up into his ribs. His reflexes moved his hand from the edge of the mask to the elbow before he could stop them. He cursed the human body's weak nervous system as the pair crashed to the bottom of the stairs.

Damian released his grip on Bertrand and rolled to his feet.

Bertrand had already recovered and launched a kick that sent Stockwell crashing into an accent table in front of the fourth-story window.

He reached behind him and grabbed an item from the table. He brought it up as a shield as the masked valet pushed his assault.

Bertrand's left fist destroyed the vase.

Shattered glass, water and daffodils showered down on Damian's head.

He grabbed another as the valet's right came crashing down. The crystal erupted and spread across the floor. The following moments were filled with a flurry of punches and the rhythm of shattering crystal, ceramic and glass while water fell and flowers filled his hair.

Stockwell soon ran out of flower receptacles. Bertrand's knuckles were bleeding profusely and laced with the shards of broken vases.

Despite this, Bertrand seemed unaffected. His pain threshold, while normally high, had seemed to rise to superhuman limits. But, now he paused. The Frenchman's chest heaved and Damian could hear muffled pants from behind the mask. Its effect seemed to have power over nerve and muscle but not over the engine that drove the body. Bertrand stood, hands up, ready, but still. He was tiring.

Stockwell looked into the dead eyes of the mask, then to the shattered remains of the vases on the floor.

Damian shrugged and tossed the remainder of a vase back on the table. "Bertrand, you will owe Mrs. Landry an apology. She is not going to be happy when she sees this mess. Really, Bertrand, this is just sloppy."

The valet burst back into action. His right foot flew above his head and came crashing towards Damian. Stockwell jumped out of the way and watched as the Frenchman's powerful leg drove through the accent table that had held the flowers.

"All right. Mask or no mask, that's coming out of your pay."

Bertrand grabbed a leg from the broken table and swung it wildly. Damian ducked, weaved and fell over multiple times dodging the swings. He scrambled backwards and stood in time to catch a foot in the chest.

Damian flew down another flight of stairs.

Bertrand jumped down the flight.

Stockwell rolled as the Frenchman's knee landed where his head had lain. He spun and swept the legs from under the possessed valet.

Bertrand landed hard on his back with little effect. He sprung to his feet and unleashed a flurry of kicks that drove Stockwell across the hall as the adventurer struggled to defend himself.

"Damn your fantastic feet, Bertrand." Damian stood with his back to the door and caught the Frenchman's left foot. The Frenchman's right foot caught him in the chest as the valet spun in the air and delivered the flying kick.

The door shattered as he flew into the trophy room.

# 4

# Welcome to America

Outside on the street, tucked into the shadows of the stairwell, the stranger watched the brownstone. It had not occurred to him that there would be no way to know if the valet had completed the job.

It was clear that it was the driver that had tried the mask and not Stockwell himself. The mask's instructions were simply to kill Stockwell. If Damian had placed it on his face, there would not have been the resulting commotion by the window.

Aside from the flurry of activity and sound of shattering glass, he could not tell what was happening in the house. He believed in the power of the mask. He dare not doubt it. But, he would have to verify Stockwell's demise before departing the city. What if the valet failed? To fail in his mission would mean death. If he couldn't prove that Stockwell had fallen, it would be better to flee than return.

He had to know. He had to enter and see the body for himself.

Stepping from the safety of the shadows, he pulled the collar of his coat high. No one knew him in this country, but the nature of his work made his palms sweat. He wasn't cut out for all of this sneaking around. In his country it just wasn't necessary. Just give him a name and a squad of several men and the name would be on a tombstone in no time. No fancy planning or trickery needed.

He darted across the street. Traffic was light, but the snow and slush concerned him. He'd never tried to move across it and had already slipped twice since arriving in the city. Hopping onto the sidewalk confirmed that his fears weren't unwarranted. His feet moved from underneath and he landed hard on his lower back and slid across the sidewalk into a pedestrian.

The man was young and toppled onto him. Arms and legs flailed as the two slid together into a pile of trash set out for collection. There they stopped.

The young man jumped to his feet. The stranger struggled to find solid footing on the frozen concrete.

"Watch where you're going, you jerk."

He wanted to apologize for his clumsiness but did not know the English words.

"First day with your new feet, ya chump?"

He got to his feet but continued to slide. He spat out apologies in Spanish as his feet shuffled back and forth.

"A foreigner? That's un-American, ya bum."

"No quise hacerte daño." He slid once more and grabbed the young man for support. With his hands on the man's collar, he finally found his balance on the ice and smiled. "Gracias."

The young man struck his hand from the jacket collar and punched the stranger in the face. The strike sent him sailing onto his back and sliding across the sidewalk.

"Lousy Greek." The young man straightened his collar and continued his walk.

The stranger sat up and stood slowly to his feet. The ice was thinner here and enough concrete broke through to make his footing sure. "Hey you, ugly American."

His English was badly broken. The accent was thick, but the young man heard. He stopped and turned. "What did you say to me, goatbanger?"

The stranger said nothing. His English was limited. The only other thing he had learned before he left for America was "you're very pretty" and it didn't seem applicable here.

"That's what I thought."

"You're very pretty, you ugly American."

"That's it. You're not even making sense but I'm going to kick your ass anyway." The young man rushed in and swung.

The stranger ducked and drove a solid fist into his stomach.

The young man let out a breath of air as he doubled over.

The stranger pulled his hand back, reached into his coat and pulled a mask identical to the one he had left in the package on the doorstep and placed it on the man's face.

Ignoring the pain in his stomach, the young man stood up straight with arms at his side. He was rigid. His anger had vanished.

The stranger smiled and leaned in close to the young man. He didn't know the English words for take a walk. But with the mask in place, he didn't have to. He whispered the instructions in Spanish into the man's ear and the man complied.

The young man turned and stepped into the street just as a truck pulled on to the avenue.

It tried to stop but slid on the ice and plowed into the young man. The thud was sickening. A woman screamed. People rushed to his aid.

They would not find the mask. It had disappeared in a puff of green smoke.

The stranger moved further down the street. No one could resist the power of the mask. If the command was to kill Stockwell, Stockwell would be killed. There was no need to check. No one could resist its control. He would just wait for the chaos that was sure to erupt when the world's second richest man was found murdered.

# 5

## The Vicious Valet

The room was clean and cold. Glass cases and marble flooring gave the room the austere atmosphere that it deserved. Along the walls and in displays were the memorabilia from Stockwell's greatest adventures. Some were as simple as uniforms crafted for the henchmen of diabolical dictators. Others were grand and domineering statues taken from their lairs. Weapon racks were everywhere and contained everything from spears and sticks to complicated advanced devices that madmen had sought to use for their purposes of world domination.

No element was out of place. Every item was kept clean and dusted thanks to the dutiful Mrs. Landry. The floor was spotless; spotless until Damian crashed through the door and sent splinters scattering across the marble.

"Seriously, man. Enough with the doors." He stood and rushed the masked valet.

Bertrand swung the table leg. It went wide. Stockwell's counterstrike caught the valet in the face. There was a thud as his fist collided with the mask. Two more quick strikes had little effect on the emotionless face. Each hit sounded with a thunk. The hollow sound puzzled Stockwell and distracted his marvelous mind long enough for the valet to land another kick.

Damian landed on his back and slid across the highly polished marble floor deep into the trophy room. He squeaked to a stop at the base of a trophy case.

Bertrand kept coming.

Damian stood and rushed in amongst the exhibits. Perhaps in the maze of displays he could gain an advantage on the machine-like man that stalked him.

Tools, weapons and vehicles of deranged madmen from across the globe filled the room. Though he appreciated the opportunity and any advantage it may provide him, it was a dangerous place to have led a possessed Frenchman wearing a creepy mask that seemed bent on killing him.

Bertrand dropped the club and moved to a weapons rack. In its display were several African spears Damian had brought back after defeating his, what the newspapers had called, "Nemesis in Natal."

The long spear cut through the air with a confusing sound. The shaft warbled like the flexing of a strip of sheet metal while the spearhead produced a shrill whistle. The combination of the two sounds made it difficult to judge the speed of the missile.

Stockwell dove for a totem pole he had saved from "The Inuit Incident" hoping the carved animals would shield him.

The tip of the spear embedded itself in the face of a smiling beaver and sheared a tooth from the carving. Stockwell tried to pull the weapon free and turn it on his murderous friend, but the blade had buried itself too deep between the beaver's over-pronounced teeth.

Bertrand threw another spear. The warble roared and the whistle screamed across the room. Stockwell slid behind a monolith that had been a key clue to the "Evil on Easter Island."

The spear struck the rock and threw off a cascade of sparks as it was deflected far out of Damian's reach.

Bertrand grabbed another spear from the rack.

Stockwell cursed himself for not bolting the weapons down or mounting a "do not throw in the house" sign on the rack itself. Weaving in and out of the various trophies, he rushed across the room. He leapt over a bed of nails from the "Insanity in India," vaulted over a pommel horse from the time he faced "The Genocidal Gymnast" and slid behind a gong that had been the centerpiece of an evil emperor's lair in "That Thingapore in Singapore." The papers weren't always clever.

The third spear struck the gong just as he stopped behind it. The sound was deafening. In the cavernous room, the ring bounced off the polished floor and metal displays. He clasped his hands over his ears and fell to the ground. Then he saw it. The reflection in a giant mirror that had once been the property of "The Vain Villain" showed Bertrand grasping at his own ears behind the mask.

Damian Stockwell kicked the gong. This sound was louder than the spear strike and sent Bertrand to the ground. He kicked it again, jumped to his feet and ran to the "Chaos in Camelot" display and grabbed a shield from a suit of armor. Behind the safety of the shield, he advanced.

The gong faded, Bertrand recovered and returned to the spear rack. He hurled one missile after another at the approaching Stockwell.

The impact of each was not slight. The shield bucked in his hand with every strike, yet he advanced quickly, deflecting spears until the South African weapons rack was all but empty.

Bertrand held the last spear in front of him and the two warriors collided.

Stockwell battered and bashed the Frenchman with the shield as the valet struck against the metal with the spear.

The weight of the shield and the force of the blows tired both combatants. Even the influence of the mask could not overcome the tremendous fatigue both men suffered.

Bertrand dropped the spear and tore the shield from Stockwell's hands. The Frenchman lowered his head and drove his shoulder into his employer, lifting him from the ground as he charged across the room.

The charge ended at the window. The sill caught Stockwell just above the waistline. His back and shoulders shattered the glass. He grabbed the mask and placed his foot on the valet's chest. A powerful shove forced the Frenchman back as the mask finally released its hold. The momentum carried Damian's arm out the broken window. His grip on the mask had been tenuous, and despite the force of the kick, it had struggled to remain in place and weakened his grip. The mask sailed out into the air above the street.

It never struck the road. It dissolved in midair. One moment the mask had been whole and hideous. The next it was a flash of green mist and it was gone.

Stockwell cursed. In his lab the mask would have revealed its secrets.

Bertrand groaned.

Damian grabbed him by the elbow and helped him stand. "Are you okay, my friend?"

"It feels like someone tried to rip my face off."

"That was me. You're welcome."

The valet looked confused as he surveyed the trophy room. Then he held up his bloodied hands. The pain began to show on his face.

"Monsieur, what is this? What happened to my hands?"

"Well, you punched a lot of glass and things."

He winced as he touched the glass shards protruding from his hands. "Mon dieu. What is going on?"

"I don't know, my loyal friend. But, we're going to find out. You'll want to tend to those hands before we head to Central America."

"Where in Central America?"

"I don't know. I was still examining the DV when you put your fist through it."

"I did what?" The Frenchman was shocked. "I remember nothing except looking at the mask in the box."

"You don't remember putting on the mask and going all Frenchy crazy on me?"

The Frenchman shook his head. He blushed to hear of his actions.

"Hmmm. I'd already deduced that the mask had an effect on your nervous system, but this sudden amnesic episode must mean that it made you stupid as well."

"I do apologize, Monsieur."

"No apologies are necessary, my friend. Aside from putting on the mask and trying to kill me, none of this is your fault. But, we must get to the bottom of this. It's a shame the mask disintegrated and took its secrets with it."

Stockwell bit his lower lip as he thought. His mind was awash with possibilities—chemical formulas, motives and cultural references flooded his mind. He needed a distraction to concentrate. Damian crossed the room and pulled a first aid kit from the shelf. Without a word, he set to removing the shards from Bertrand's hands. Exercising caution to prevent nerve damage, he tweezed and stitched each laceration until the valet's hands were clear of debris. He treated the wounds and wrapped the hands. By the time he was done, he had formulated a plan.

"Bertrand, call the club and see if Williams is in."

Bertrand held up his hands. The gauze wrapped his hand with the thickness of a boxer's gloves. "Monsieur, how should I call?"

Stockwell rolled his eyes. "Use the phone, Bertrand. You shouldn't be such a luddite."

Bertrand sighed. "Oui, Monsieur."

"Oh, and while you're on the phone, call down to the warehouse and have them prep the plane. We'll be flying out today."

"Oui, Monsieur. May I trouble you for a pen?"

Damian pulled a pen from his pocket. "It's not that much to remember, Bertrand."

"Non. I just need it to dial." Bertrand gripped the pen in his teeth.

Stockwell shook his head and laughed, "Ah, you French. So weird."

Bertrand mumbled something. The pen in his mouth made it hard to understand. He turned to leave the room.

Stockwell called him back. "Bertrand."

The Frenchman turned.

"It's good to have you back on my side, my friend."

Bertrand smiled, nodded and disappeared into the stairwell.

Stockwell turned his attention out the window. What could have caused the mask to evaporate like that? And what was that flash of green?

He had seen the flash of green from across the street. And, once he saw his target lean out the window, he knew his plan had failed.

How could the mask have failed? Fear crept into him as he realized that he may have to face this legend himself. He tried to shake the feeling as he walked down the street to where he had parked. Before getting into the driver's seat, he moved around to the trunk and withdrew a large case.

He sat the case next to him in the passenger's seat and opened it. There were four masks left. Four chances that he would not have to try and kill Damian Stockwell himself.

# 6

## Hey, Lady

The valet had been beaten. Everything he knew about the Frenchman had made the man the world's best candidate to defeat Damian Stockwell. His skills and proximity had made him the perfect choice to don the mask. But, he had failed. If he wasn't strong enough to beat the famed adventurer, who would be?

The foreigner had driven through the streets of New York aimlessly, looking for someone strong enough to beat the man that many cultures called the White Demon. After an hour, it became clear that only a circus strongman may possess the strength necessary and there were none strolling the streets this day.

He had all but resigned himself to performing the murder himself. A cold spot had begun to form in his stomach. His hand shook when he raised it to wipe the nervous sweat from his brow. Fear had been in the back of his mind ever since he had received the dossier that held Stockwell's name. Now it grew as he turned and drove back towards the townhouse to perform the hit himself.

The closer he got, the worse he shook. He was a block away when the shaking forced him to pull over.

The sedan lurched as he pulled to the curb. His shaking hand found the window crank and turned furiously. Cold air rushed into the car and beat back the sweat that had begun to drip down his face.

He took slow, deep breaths and whispered comforting things to himself.

He reminded himself that he had killed plenty of men—that this was no different. But his instincts could not be convinced. Damian Stockwell was no ordinary man. He was a legend.

He leaned closer to the cold air that drifted in through the window. He had never known a winter this cold—the dry air was as foreign to him as the cold itself. He was accustomed to dampness, and longed for the humidity of his home's still air. Still, its chill was comforting and the air carried something more.

The sound was unmistakable. It was a voice that sounded his deliverance. The words were sweet to his desperate ears.

"Yeah, baby. Shake that ass!"

The sound had come from around the corner. He leapt from the car, cautious this time of his footing, and ran to the street's corner.

What he saw caused him to smile. There were four of them and they were perfect.

Each man was burlier than the last, if arranged in the proper order. Their faces were chiseled and tanned. Their muscles were massive and toned. Their sandwiches were ham and cheese.

The four men sat perched on a stack of bricks with their lunches spread across their laps. Steel thermoses sat uncapped and at the ready. The biggest man was the one with the voice. The brute would point at a woman walking by, lean in to his coworkers, whisper something and then shout.

A long-legged brunette was his next target.

"Whoa, baby! With legs like that you should be in pictures. Or my bed."

She huffed and quickened her pace.

He shouted after her, "My bed pays better than pictures."

The others did not join in on the catcalls. They would only laugh and encourage his comments. They'd help choose his targets and try not to choke on their ham and cheese sandwiches as he insulted nearly every woman who passed the construction site. The women did their best not to respond and simply hurried on their way.

This only encouraged the men.

A woman carrying a stack of books received, "Hey, baby. Wanna teach me how to read ... in my bed?"

Another woman strolled by with her dog and drew a comment.

"Whoa, girl. You could put me on a leash ... in my bed."

A tall blonde, her arms filled with shopping bags, grabbed his attention.

"What's in the bags, baby? Uh ... in my bed."

The calls were usually attribute specific but he had a standard list of calls for those that fit no particular profile.

"Yo, Momma! Wanna see my pile driver?" With this he pointed to the site's pile driver. Variations of this played out with sledgehammer, iron girder, jackhammer, fire hose and four-ton crane—basically anything big and long.

The foreigner watched them from the corner of the building.

The men sat beneath the framework of a skyscraper in progress. These steel-skeletoned giants seemed to spring from the city like ironweeds. As the city had grown on the world stage, it had grown in height and the buildings of the great metropolis dreamt of touching the stars like the citizens themselves.

The men had no doubt help set the steel, haul the bricks and drive the rivets that kept the building still in the high winds of its great heights. Together these men had swung hammers, wielded rivet guns and carted wheelbarrows full of bricks. And, together, they would defeat the White Demon.

He reached into the bag and pulled out one of the remaining masks.

"Hey, honey. Those legs go all the way up?" The large man chuckled as his lunch-mates laughed.

"Yes, they do, asshole!" the random target fired back.

The simple fact that she had responded startled the man. Bullies were never prepared for a strong target. Perhaps because he was convinced it was true, or simply to save face, the worker shot back, "That's friggin' weird, lady."

He stepped over a barricade and walked towards the men who were still chuckling. "Pardon."

One of the other workers spoke up, "What's with the accent?"

The others joined in.

"Doesn't sound like you're from around here."

"He talks funny."

The largest of the men turned his attention from insulting women and dropped to the ground. He walked over to the foreigner and pointed. "What do you want, little man?"

Little? He was a tall man in his own country. But, standing before this mountain of a man, he did feel small. Regardless of his stature, he had always been quick. Before the rest of the crew could set their thermoses aside, he struck the man in the stomach The large construction worker doubled over and the little man placed the mask on the worker's face.

The other three were now on their feet.

"What do you think you're doing, señor?"

"Leave Tommy alone."

"You got a lot of nerve coming to our country and slapping a mask on a guy when he's entertaining the ladies like that, fella."

Tommy, for his part, stood quiet and still.

The other three workers surrounded the foreigner.

He said nothing, but reached calmly into the satchel and pulled out another mask.

One of the laborers grabbed him by the collar. Tommy sprung to life and grabbed the laborer by the arm.

"Tommy, let go. This guy's a creep."

Tommy said nothing. He squeezed.

"Geez, Tommy. You're breaking my wrist."

The laborer let go of the foreigner's collar and turned his attention to Tommy. He tried to pry the hand from his wrist, but the iron grip would not give.

The other two jumped in to help. The smallest large man grabbed Tommy around the neck while the other tried to help pull his friend's wrist free.

The foreigner smiled as he watched the situation unfold.

Tommy had shifted his weight forward and thrown the man from his back to the ground. The man landed with a thud and gasp. He received the next mask.

With silent obedience, the construction worker stood from the ground and took a mask from the foreigner. He placed it on his friend.

The last worker was still caught in Tommy's grip.

"What did you do to them? What did you do to my friends?"

The foreigner said nothing. He pulled the last mask from the satchel and stepped forward.

The worker spit in his face—a useless act of defiance. The three masked construction workers grabbed him and pulled him to the ground.

"You bastard. What are you doing? What do you want?"

He leaned in close with the mask and smiled. "You kill Damian Stockwell."

# 7

## Detour of Doom

He had found both his suit and his valet laid out in his room. The suit was in the center of the colossal four-poster bed. Bertrand was in the center of the floor.

Stockwell crossed quickly to the medicine cabinet and retrieved a vile of smelling salts. A person fainting in his bedroom was not an uncommon occurrence and he was fully prepared for the event. That it was a man that had collapsed … now that was different.

Damian waved the putrid smelling odor under Bertrand's nose. The Frenchman's face twitched, but he did not wake. He waved the sal volatile once more beneath the valet's ample nose. The twitch was larger but he still did not rouse.

He pocketed the salts and slapped Bertrand hard across the face.

"Zut alors!" The valet sat straight up and swung at Stockwell.

Damian dodged the reflexive strike and grabbed his friend's shoulder.

"My friend, you passed out. I fear it is the loss of blood."

Bertrand raised his hand to his head. He winced at the pain and looked at his hand. Thickly bandaged, the Frenchman was shocked to see blood trickling from the dressing. "It should have stopped by now."

"Damn the cloud of green." Stockwell stood and began to pace the room. "This is no doubt an effect of the mask. Had it not disintegrated, I would know more about the cursed thing."

Bertrand grabbed the edge of the bed and pulled himself slowly to his feet.

"Bertrand, you shouldn't do that."

"Non, Monsieur. It is okay. I have the strength."

"No, I meant grab the sheets like that. You're bleeding like a stuck French pig, um, uh, cochon. And those sheets are Egyptian cotton."

"My apologies, Monsieur." Bertrand released his grip and sat back on the floor.

Stockwell offered his hand and helped pull him to his feet. "Dahlia picked them out."

Bertrand struggled to stand. "They are nice sheets, Monsieur."

Stockwell waved his comment off, "It's just … that … you know … women."

"Oui, Monsieur. Women."

They each forced a laugh since neither understood the joke. Bertrand doubled over. Stockwell, moving with an unexpected speed, caught the Frenchman and eased him onto the bed. His friend was weak.

"I'm sorry, Monsieur. It must be the losing of the blood."

"Of course it is, my friend. I'm sure it had nothing to do with me beating you soundly this morning."

"I don't remember that."

"Well, you were wearing the mask and all. But, it was pretty impressive."

The proud Frenchman hung his head.

"Hey, there's no need for that, Bertrand. You were pretty good too. You were all kicks and punches and, my God, you hate vases." Stockwell laughed.

Bertrand did not respond.

"Come on now. Chin up." Damian lifted the Frenchman's chin. "We'll find Simmons and there will be plenty of people to defeat. You'll feel better. There's no need to mope."

Bertrand's eyes were closed.

"Oh, you've passed out again."

Stockwell set his friend back into the bed and checked his vitals. Assured that his friend was just resting, he grabbed the suit from his bed, the luggage from the door and stepped into the master bath.

He returned to the room, called his private doctor and arranged for him to tend to Bertrand. He hung up the phone and stepped into the wardrobe.

He dressed quickly in durable, loose-fit clothing and pulled his wallet from a drawer. These actions, though seemingly meaningless, had armed him for anything that the forces behind the demon mask could muster. Inside each piece of clothing was hidden an assortment of tools and weapons that even the most perverse frisker would have trouble detecting.

Damian opened one final drawer and withdrew a .45 automatic. The pistol was polished to a mirror finish. Even in the low light of the closet, it gleamed. Some tools needed to be seen. He dropped the weapon into his duffel bag and made his way to the garage.

Stockwell kept an extensive collection of automobiles at his downtown warehouse but always had two on hand in the brownstone's garage. The polished Duesy sat in stark contrast next to the marred body panels of a Model B Ford. Dents and scratches went unattended with intent. In fact, many of the blemishes had been placed on the car's body intentionally. Mechanically, the Model B's V-8 received no less attention than the Duesenberg's or any other car in his collection. The engine had been reworked. Stockwell had spent hours over the disassembled engine block fine-tuning its performance. He had tripled the output to nearly two hundred horsepower and there were few cars on any kind of road that could pass the Model B.

Even with its powerful drivetrain, the outward appearance was its greatest asset. Like a fine disguise, the car's blemished body served as camouflage enabling it to hide amidst the cars of the city. No one would look twice at the Ford expecting to see one of the world's wealthiest men behind the wheel.

Stockwell flicked a switch on the garage wall. A whir filled the room as the garage door rose. He tossed the duffel into the back of the Ford and fired the powerful engine. First gear was engaged with no resistance. The transmission had seen as much work as the engine. He rolled forward into the alley.

Behind him, the door would reach its apex, hang for a moment and close automatically. His lawyers were working on the patent.

The Ford pulled from the alleyway and blended into traffic like a plumber in a hotel lobby.

The March sun passed through the Ford's dirty windshield. Winter had clung to New York like a needy child that would just stand there in front of their parents with their arms outstretched and saying, "Up, up." The roads were clear but the banks had yet to melt away completely.

Stockwell had pulled out of the alleyway to find his southward path blocked by construction barricades. There were no workers present but it wasn't unlike the city to place barricades ahead of the work.

He turned north up the street and planned to double back to the club. Bertrand had called and was informed that Williams would be in for the afternoon. If anyone knew where Simmons had ventured, it would be the club's outfitter.

A block down, he turned right and the city rose up in front of him. New York had grown at a ridiculous rate before the depression. Even now it seemed as if some new high-rise was going up on every corner. Stretched across the city were the frames of new buildings. American steel was building American landmarks at an astounding pace. He smiled—proud to be a part of the American dream.

The next southbound street was barricaded as well.

Damian's suspicions were triggered. He was one of the world's smartest men but even he knew that his guts were to be trusted over the mind's weak rationalizations. Several times he had been forced to disregard reason and logic and embrace an unscientific, unexplainable feeling from deep inside himself.

On all but one of the occasions, trusting his instincts had saved his life. The other time led to a moment of great embarrassment and a potential international incident. In the end, the diplomat had gotten his clothes back and all was well.

This was different, however. The construction barriers seemed to be directing him. Leading him into a trap. He decided to let the trap play out. He'd play their game. The mask's self-destruction had robbed him of the only clue to its mysterious origins and unexplainable control over Bertrand. He would play right into their hands. Then he would grab their hands and make the perpetrators punch themselves in the face until they told him what he wanted to know.

The barricades forced him south at the next intersection. They obviously weren't trying to keep him from his club. They were leading him somewhere else.

He could see no other barricades on the road in front of him. The trap must be on the street. He would be vigilant.

The foreigner almost missed Stockwell. He hadn't necessarily expected the Duesenberg, but the Model B had been a surprise. He would have missed his target completely had it not been for the blond man's striking appearance.

Even concealed within the Model B's cabin, women pointed and swooned as he passed by.

The commotion had drawn the assassin's attention just as the Ford made its first turn. Stockwell did not appear to find the barricades suspicious. He smiled.

# 8

## Construction Catastrophe

Traffic had been moving smoothly until Damian reached the construction site. There it slowed as the cars moved around a jackhammer operator in the middle of the street. Cabs and trucks rolled past him as Stockwell inched the Ford forward, waiting for an opening in the adjacent lane.

While waiting for his chance to merge, he began to concentrate on the mask. Since Bertrand had been throwing punches and spears at him, Stockwell hadn't been able to study the mask's features for more than a few moments. Still, he had trained his mind to turn quick glimpses into detailed images. It required tremendous concentration and silence, so sitting in New York traffic in front of a jackhammer made the process more difficult.

He pulled his lower lip into his teeth, chewing gently. Despite the hammer, he was intent on remembering the details of the mask that had possessed his valet and forced him into a bloodthirsty rage. He closed his eyes.

The features of the horrid face began to appear in his mind. Black, soulless eyes were at the heart of the nightmare. Creased brows dove inward to the bridge of a wide nose giving the mask an angry appearance. Pointed cheekbones drove up into the eye sockets. Large, cracked teeth filled the giant maw of a mouth. At first he had remembered the mask as a single color but now his mind's eye's memory revealed that he had been mistaken. Greens, reds and yellows were present on the mask, but they were not bold. The colors were washes—muted and swallowed by the texture of the mask itself.

The mask had clearly formed in his mind. He would never forget the image now. Though, he hoped to never see it again.

Stockwell realized the jackhammer had stopped.

He opened his eyes.

The mask was staring at him. The same horrific mask that Bertrand had donned was now set beneath the hard hat of the jackhammer operator.

Damian's eyes narrowed trying to pierce through the black lens that blocked the construction worker's eyes. Then he saw it. A flash of light rippled across the soulless eyes of the mask and the man sprang onto the hood of the Model B wielding the jackhammer.

He drove the bit into the hood of the car and activated the pneumatic ram. The steel bit tore through the hood and engine block before Damian could put the car into gear.

Stockwell pulled open the door only to have it forced shut by a pile of bricks. Another worker, in another mask, had plowed the wheelbarrow full of masonry into the door. Stockwell lunged for the passenger door as the worker on the hood leapt onto the roof of the coupe.

Damian slid across the bench seat just as the bit of the jackhammer plunged through the steel and perforated the roof.

Instinctively he drew his weapon and pointed it at the roof. He hesitated, reminding himself that these men were under the control of the mask and not their own conscious mind. Though they were trying to kill him, they were not the enemy. He holstered the 1911. He would have to stop them with his bare and mighty fists.

The bit drove through the roof again, missing Stockwell's shoulder by mere inches. Another crash sounded from the passenger door. A cement mixer had been rolled into the street and now barricaded him into the car.

Stockwell rolled into the backseat as the construction worker on the roof probed the front end of the Ford with the powerful jackhammer.

The rear window exploded and covered Stockwell with glass. The sledge that had destroyed the window swung again. This time it was aiming for his head. He dropped to the floorboards as the front windshield exploded and a hose was thrown into the car. The smell of gasoline was unmistakable. He didn't have much time before they would ignite the car.

The sledge continued to swing through the windshield in wide arcs. The jackhammer dove in and out of the cabin with growing speed. But, its points of entry were becoming systematic and predictable.

Damian could feel the fuel soaking into his shirt. It wouldn't be long now. He had to act.

The jackhammer retreated. The sledge swung. He drove his right leg up and caught the hammer's head with his foot, wedging it between the roof and his powerful legs.

The jackhammer drove through the roof and into the head of the sledge. The massive vibrations shook the sledge from the wielder's hand. Damian didn't let the hammer fall; he caught it flat with his left foot and held it against the roof.

He felt the jackhammer operator begin to withdraw the pneumatic tool. He knew the operator had to be tiring. He had punched dozens of holes into the roof of the car and the physical strength it took to lift the hammer from an unstable surface was about to work in Stockwell's favor.

Protected by the thick head of the sledge, Damian drove his left leg up to the roof of the car as the chisel tip entered. The unexpected resistance forced the jackhammer into the operator's chin. Damian saw the worker above him fall to the ground and heard the idling jackhammer bounce around the roof.

Two of his assailants were now unarmed. He had to move.

Stockwell rolled into a crouch. A glowing rivet landed on the rear seat. The red hot metal sank into the fabric and began to smolder.

Damian dove as flames began to dance. He launched himself through the shattered remnants of the rear window. Glass shred fabric and flesh but he cleared the car as the rivet's flame ignited the spilled fuel.

The Model B, lovingly made to look like crap, exploded as Stockwell rolled across the concrete. The blast shattered nearby windows. The men in the masks reached to cover their ears. Like Bertrand in the trophy room, the sound had weakened the masks' hold on them.

Unfortunately, there was no time to exploit the situation.

Flames spilled around him as he dove for cover. His fear was not so much the explosion but the fuel soaked clothing he was now wearing. He rolled again to subdue any flames that may have formed. Content that he was not on fire, he stood and charged back on to the street.

Any effect the explosion had on the workers had worn off. Damian figured that the mask's control dominated not only the conscious mind but other subconscious functions as well. Much like it dulled Bertrand's pain, the control elicited also controlled the person's balance. It wasn't as if their balance needed aid. These men's lives and livelihood depended on their ability to walk the narrow beams and girders of the iron giants they constructed. But, heightened by the mask's control, they would be almost impossible to throw. Judo was out. The ability to use leverage against these men would be not unlike trying to throw a wall over one's shoulder. He would have to meet brute force with the same.

It would be clenched fists versus the iron tools and sinew of the men who were building America—good men, no doubt, when the effects of the mask did not possess them.

It was a remarkable device to say the least. And it held answers. Damian Stockwell strode back into the fray, determined to defeat the men set against him and retrieve one of the demon tiki masks intact.

The man that had shattered the rear window was closest to him. His sledge taken, the man had pulled a large wrench from his tool belt.

Damian could not strike the mask for fear of activating the self-destructive flash of green. The man's head was protected by a hardhat; his body was covered in a thick canvas jumpsuit. Even his fingers were protected deep within thick canvas gloves.

The only exposed part of his body was his throat which lay behind the flashing chrome of the wrench.

The man wielded the tool with the precision of an experienced knife fighter. The wrench whistled by Damian's head as he ducked, the tool's motions driving him closer to the burning hulk of the Ford.

Any closer to the car and his fuel soaked clothing would combust. He had to change the direction of the fight.

Stockwell rolled under a wide swing and came to his feet beside the man. He dove for the worker's neck.

The worker was quick with his backhand. The base of the wrench caught Damian on the cheek and forced him to the ground. Had he not been so close to the worker, the head of the tool would have struck him unconscious.

He ducked under a swing and struck back. He landed several punches in succession in the man's midsection. Each drove air from the man's lungs but was unaccompanied by the familiar grunt that came with the pain of being struck in the abdomen. Stockwell was sure that the final punch of the combination broke a rib but, again, there was no sign of pain or effect. The mask's control was final, right down to the man's nervous system.

The foot of a steel-toed boot crashed into Damian's chest and threw him back onto the ground. He used the momentum to roll further away from the fire.

His hands were screaming. Holding them before his eyes, he could see that the furious blows he had administered against the canvas jumpsuit had shredded his knuckles.

The worker moved towards him unabated. The jackhammer operator had moved in behind him holding a screwdriver like a killer's stiletto. The worker that had dumped the pallet of bricks had been thrown back by the car's blast and was just now getting to his feet. His arm was on fire.

Stockwell had to help. The mask's pain killing effect could leave the man disfigured or handicapped for life—if it didn't kill him first. He had to move fast.

He dodged a stab from the screwdriver and drove his shoulder into the construction worker. Even a superhuman sense of balance is useless to a man when his feet are no longer beneath him. The worker was driven from the ground and into a swing of the wrench.

Stockwell moved from under the falling man and rushed toward the flaming worker. He couldn't get near the man to help him without risking bursting into flames himself.

The worker saw him through the soulless black eyes of the mask and started towards him. He had no weapon other than his flaming arm. He rushed towards Stockwell; air fueled the fire as it spread to the elbow.

Damian backed away.

The worker swung his arm widely, enraging the flames. Strikes flew by Damian's head, threatening to ignite his jacket. There was no time to remove the coat. There was barely time to back away.

He risked a glance behind him and found what he needed. A thick water hose sat on the ground next to a cement mixer.

Stockwell backed towards the mixer and allowed the man on fire to get closer.

It seemed a single focus to apply the burning arm to Stockwell's jacket. The man struck only with his right arm. Still, the punches came fast, each missing Damian's head by inches.

A quick series of strikes came. On the third strike, Stockwell made his move. In one fluid motion he spun to his right and dropped the lever on the cement mixer. He had positioned himself right in front of the spinning device.

The force of the punch carried the worker's fist deep into the mixing cement.

The fire was doused. The man was stuck.

Stockwell had no desire to remove the man's arm, so he hit the switch on the mixer and stopped the blades from turning. The worker became focused on pulling his arm from the slurry of the cement.

Stockwell reached for the mask, hoping to remove it without the green mist taking another clue from him. But, as soon as he got close, the worker turned and stared at him through the dead eyes. The black lenses rippled quickly from the tear duct outward and the worker's efforts changed. He stopped trying to remove his right arm from the mixer and began grabbing for Stockwell with his left. He grabbed Damian by the collar.

Stockwell looked back into black void of the eyes and saw movement in the reflection of the mask. He pulled his knees to his chest and placed his full weight on the worker's outstretched arm. The grip may not give. But, even a man possessed could not hold Damian's concentrated weight at arm's length.

Stockwell hit the ground the instant the board struck the mask in the face. The board exploded, the mask disintegrated and the worker fell unconscious with his arm stuck in the cement mixer.

Stockwell dove under the mixer and came up on the other side. Wrench and Screwdriver had caught up. Screwdriver had swung the board intending to finish him. Now the worker lunged over the mixer. Stockwell grabbed his coveralls and pulled him along.

The man tumbled over the mixer and Damian made a grab for the mask. It slid off the worker's face and into his hand.

"Ha." Stockwell held it up to examine it. But, it was only there for a moment. A green mist enshrouded the mask and it disappeared before his very eyes. "Damn!"

Stockwell pulled his hand back. The mist had burned his fingers like scalding water.

There was a clunk, a clang and a ping from the mixer.

The man with the wrench left dents in the mixer barrel as he cleaved at the air.

A burning rivet landed in the dirt at Damian's feet. It was only now that Stockwell saw the fourth worker up in the structure itself. Several stories up, the man stood near the rivet furnace with a pair of tongs and hurled a third rivet towards him.

The searing red bolt flew directly at his head. He ducked in time and scrambled from behind the mixer. He had to end this before he burst into flames.

He moved deeper into the construction site as the worker with the wrench ran to keep up. Damian ran deftly up a pile of lumber as the worker scrambled after him.

He reached the top of the pile and leapt for an exposed girder.

The worker reached the top of the pile.

Damian kicked him in the shoulder and spun the worker around. Hanging from the girder, he locked his legs around the man's neck and lifted him from the ground.

It was a risky move. He didn't want to break the man's neck, but as he had figured, the mask saw an opportunity to kill Stockwell and the worker dropped the wrench and grabbed Damian's legs. The masked worker began to kick and spin, trying desperately to pull Stockwell from the girder.

But Damian's grip was firm. He raised his legs and pulled the massive construction worker closer. He wanted a closer look at the mask's fastening system. There had to be something, a trigger or relay that caused the mask to self-destruct when removed.

He saw nothing. There was no strap holding the mask in place.

For the first time, Stockwell thought that maybe there was something more to these masks. Something mystical. His inner skeptic had always served him well, but now he began to doubt that his skepticism could be trusted.

The worker began to kick harder—using his weight to try and tear Stockwell from the girder.

Damian twisted the grip on his legs. His knee roughly bumped the mask. There was a slight hiss and it fell from the worker's face. It was gone before it hit the ground. Only a green mist floated in the air.

The worker stopped struggling and looked up at Damian. "Who are you? What's going on?"

"My name is Damian Stockwell and you're about to have a minor fall."

Stockwell released the construction worker and the man collapsed down upon the stack of lumber. The distance was not great and only resulted in a twisted ankle.

Damian released the girder and dropped to the ground beside him.

Tommy writhed in pain. "What did you drop me for?"

"I didn't want to break your neck."

"What the hell is going on here? Last thing I remember is looking at some hot little dish."

"You and your friends have been under the influence of another. You've spent the last few minutes drilling holes in my car and trying to kill me."

The man's face said it all. He had no recollection of the fight. "That's a little hard to swallow, mister."

"Maybe, but you've been an unwilling pawn in a madman's game. A game called Kill Damian Stockwell."

"Whatever you say, lunatic."

"Are you sure you don't remember anything else?"

Tommy thought for a moment. It was obvious the process took some concentration. "Nah, that's all. Well, I remember a flash of light. That's it."

Stockwell nodded. "One of your friends is stuck in the cement mixer. The other should be laid out behind it. Get them to safety and call this number." He handed Tommy a card. "Tell them everything you remember. They'll also cover any injuries you incurred while getting your ass kicked by me."

Tommy looked at the card. It simply said 1.

"What's this?"

"That's my phone number. A Frenchman will answer. Be nice."

"Man, that's not a real number."

"It is. I'm number one."

With this, Stockwell rushed back up the pile of lumber and leapt to the girder. He pulled himself up and made his way into the framework of the high-rise.

There was one mask left.

No. It couldn't be! How had he managed to defeat the workers? With the aid of the masks, these brutish thugs had been brought to peak levels of strength and endurance. They should have been unbeatable.

He watched from above as Stockwell tore apart the three construction workers. There was still the fourth up in the girders, but what chance did one have where three had failed?

He couldn't wait. He would have to kill Stockwell himself. Unzipping the satchel in full, he revealed a secret compartment that housed the separate components of a deadly sniper rifle. He crouched on the makeshift plywood flooring of the fifth story and set to assembling the weapon. He hoped to have a clear shot before Stockwell reached the riveter.

●●●

Stockwell ran along the girders of the first story and took a series of rickety ladders to the fourth. He hesitated at the foot of the ladder to the fifth floor.

He knew the riveter would be expecting him and, considering his accuracy from the fifth floor, the man would be unable to miss at such close range. Damian had little choice. There was only one way up. He quickly devised a ridiculous plan, removed his fuel-soaked jacket and rushed up the ladder.

He rolled onto the plywood base of the fifth floor. A rivet flew over him. Had he been standing it would have struck his head. He didn't expect it to be long before the second rivet flew.

Stockwell leapt to his feet and draped his jacket out like a matador's cape daring the bull, taunting the beast.

The second rivet was already on the way.

Stockwell caught the near-molten metal in the folds of his jacket. He spun like the matador, balled the coat around the red-hot rivet and threw the garment at the riveter.

The jacket flew towards the worker and burst into flames.

As the fireball approached him, the riveter brought his arms up to shield himself. Aided by the rushing air, the fuel soaked jacket burned quickly. It was all but threads and embers when it landed on the masked construction worker. The fire had consumed itself in a flash. The jacket was all but harmless, but, unfortunately for the riveter, Stockwell was right behind it.

Damian dove into the man and drove him against a steel column. The worker lunged forward with surprising speed, but Stockwell was quicker. He caught the man by the neck and drove his head into the steel, knocking the worker unconscious. The man's body dropped to the floor. The mask was still intact.

Stockwell finally had a chance to examine this devil's mask without the wearer trying to kill him. This, he knew, would make the examination easier.

Damian leaned in close. The face on the mask was similar to the others. The expression was horrid, like a man in pain trapped in wood. But, was it wood?

There was a grain on the mask, but, as Damian studied it, he realized it looked unnatural. It was too consistent. Damian reached slowly to touch the mask, careful not to disrupt its hold on the worker's face.

The report triggered his reflexes and he pulled back his hand.

The sniper's bullet shattered the outside edge of the mask. It didn't splinter; it shattered. The green mist hissed from the bullet hole.

Stockwell reacted with haste. In one move he swiped the mask from the unconscious worker's face. The man had been spared the bullet; he did not need to suffer burns caused by the mist. He grabbed the worker's belt and rolled them both off the edge of the fifth floor.

A second bullet splintered the plywood a moment later.

Stockwell's shoulder wrenched in pain as he caught the bottom edge of a girder. The extra weight of the worker caused a tremendous jar on his arm and he struggled to hold the edge with a single hand.

"Throw him!"

Stockwell looked to the ground below him. Tommy and the other two workers were dragging a large tarp into position below him.

"Just make sure he clears that girder!"

The three set up in a triangle around the canvas and pulled it taught.

"We've got him, Mr. Stockwell! Just toss him this way."

The jarring catch had robbed him of any momentum. He had to build up a swing. And, he had to hurry. He could sense the sniper repositioning.

One mighty swing and he heaved the listless body of the construction worker into the air. The unconscious man cleared the girder with ease and the men on the ground scrambled back to place the canvas under their plummeting friend.

He landed with an anticlimactic whump. The tarp broke the fall and the workers began to move to safety behind a pile of bricks.

Damian drew his Colt, kicked his legs and dropped to the girders of the third floor. He charged with nimble feet, balancing without effort across the ribs of the steel skeleton. He leapt across spans that would have caused experienced high walkers to pause and made his way closer to the sniper's position.

Rifle rounds screamed by him and ricocheted off the steel so close that it would appear to the men below that Stockwell's speed alone was causing the sparks at his heels.

As he neared the sniper's nest the rounds were fired with haste. Accuracy waned as the shooter traded care for speed. The sniper was beginning to panic.

Damian reached the ladder, struck two rungs and propelled himself to the fourth floor. He ascended the next two floors quickly and arrived at the sniper's previous position.

The assassin was a coward. He had hidden behind the innocent. He had struck from a distance. Now he ran.

As Stockwell gained his footing, the rifle clattered to the plywood flooring. The assassin backed toward the edge of the building.

"You cad!" Damian brought his Colt to bear on the man. "You corrupt others to bring harm. There is no fouler kind of criminal than the coward. Now, we're going to talk about this voodoo mask of yours."

The assassin stepped from the edge into nothing.

# 9

## Leap of Faith

His name was Billy Coldwell and he had just been hurled from a building ledge into a tarp. Woozy and bewildered, he emerged from a state that he couldn't quite explain. His mind felt as if it were fogged over. Recalling the last few moments was difficult. There had been movement—that much he could recall. Muscles ached as though he had been exerting himself but the last thing he could remember was a coworker offering him a hand and pulling him from a canvas tarp.

Taking the nearest hand, he stood on weak legs. His coworkers were shouting about something. Had he heard gunfire? Hands waved frantically at him as his coworkers screamed, but their voices were muted. The sounds around him echoed. The headache was worse than a hangover.

His friends' motions were becoming broader. They wouldn't stop screaming.

Billy took a deep breath. Clarity rushed back to him. Time was still missing but sound became clearer. That was a gunshot. His friends were ushering him to safety.

"Move, Billy!"

"Get over here, you dumb bastard!"

Awash with awareness, his predicament became clear. His friends were taking cover behind a pallet of bricks. Panic told him to join them. He was finally in control of himself and he moved to take shelter.

That's when the assassin landed on him.

The man Stockwell had thrown to safety had barely gained his footing when the assassin crushed him to the ground in a selfish attempt to break his own fall.

Damian heard the pain in the man's gasp as he was driven back to the ground.

The assassin rolled from the once again unconscious man and struggled to his feet. Injury would be all but impossible to avoid from such a fall and it showed in the criminal's gait. An obvious limp slowed the man and the still conscious construction workers looked to take advantage of the weakness as the three men emerged from their pile of bricks.

Damian held courage as the most admirable trait a man could possess, but he cursed the workers as they had placed themselves between the villain and his Colt.

The men closed on the criminal. He was confident they would detain their manipulator, but he feared that their gruff nature may cause them to dish out justice on a level so harsh that the perpetrator would be unfit to answer questions.

He needed to intervene quickly.

A rope dangled several feet out over the construction site. He could not discern its purpose—its anchor was out of site somewhere high in the structure. It could be nothing more than an unsecured rope left carelessly dangling over an edge or it could be run through a pulley and attached to a hefty load capable of bearing his weight.

Stockwell leapt.

He felt frayed fibers dig into his palm as his body, momentarily parallel to the ground, brought its full weight to bear on his grip and the rope. The impact was minimized when the rope did not completely hold his weight.

His decent was rapid but not without resistance. The rope was run through a system of pulleys. Whatever load sat on the other end did not equal his weight, but was significant enough to slow his descent.

The ground approached; he looked back to the would-be assassin and the construction workers. They were closing in on the stranger.

The largest worker, Tommy, struck first. He held the shovel in his hand like a baseball bat and looked more than capable of giving any pitch a ride. The blade, coated thick with wet cement, was heavy and would be impossible to deflect. If the villain could not dodge the strike, he would be in a coma for weeks and of little use to Stockwell's investigation.

The assassin made no attempt to dodge. Instead he dug into his coat and pulled out a weapon. It resembled a gun only from the presence of a grip and a barrel. Large cylinders were mounted under and behind the barrel. Piping of some manner led from these to what he could only call the breach.

When the trigger was pulled, the weapon didn't go "bang," it went "kachunk."

A green mist exploded on the head of the shovel. Physics seemed inapplicable. The shot did not drive the shovel back or strike it from the construction worker's hands; it simply dissolved the blade into nothing. Like the green mist that had stolen the secret of the masks from him, the shot caused the head of the shovel to disintegrate.

Twice more the deep "kachunk" of the weapon sounded as the construction workers scrambled back behind the pallet of bricks.

A fourth shot removed a quarter of the stack as it turned the kiln-fired brick into a green sludge that slowly oozed to the ground.

The perpetrator took aim again.

"Coward!" Damian screamed. He now cursed his slow descent—safety be damned, he needed to be on the ground now.

The shout had drawn the villain's attention and he turned the contraption on Damian. The green mist flew at him like a blast from a hose—emerald wisps coiled around the stream of acid and quickly dissipated into an ethereal green fog.

Damian tried to scramble lower down the rope, but every time he let go, the weighted ropes pulled back up. Through tremendous effort, he was able to lower himself only a couple of feet. It wasn't much but it was enough that the acidic volley missed his hands and coated the rope above him.

There was no sizzle, no foam of reaction, the rope did not fray and stress. The section of the rope coated with the green liquid simply disappeared as he watched.

Gravity took hold of the giant man and yanked him to the ground. The fall was thirty feet, a distance he had survived many times, but the last ten was through a stack of shipping pallets. Cedar boards splintered as his body crashed through the pile.

Damian Stockwell tore his way out of the collapsed stack of wood and twisted nails. He grunted, threw the bulk of the pile from him and turned to face the villain.

He was gone. Vanished like an object struck by the mysterious contraption that had melted the brick and disintegrated the rope. Stockwell ran into the construction yard half expecting to see a shroud of green mist where the man had stood. But there was nothing.

"What foul mixture of science and wizardry is this? How can a man just vanish?"

# 10

## Just Another Vagabond

Apparently the man had not just vanished. No, he had walked away slowly. The construction crew explained how Damian had been struck unconscious for a brief moment when he collapsed through the pallets and the criminal had limped off into the streets of New York.

Tommy continued to catch Stockwell up, "Oh, and I called your number. It took the guy forever to answer."

Damian nodded. "Bertrand has had a rough day. I kicked his ass this morning and I think it hurt his pride a bit."

"Yeah and he was pretty hard to understand. Is he retarded or something?"

Stockwell nodded. "No, he's French."

One of the others spoke up, "I've got a cousin that's a retard. He sounds French."

Damian ignored the remark, "What did Bertrand say?"

"He said that he would be on his way soon."

Stockwell looked at his watch and to the street. He then shook his head. "When he gets here, tell him to never mind."

"When he gets here tell him to never mind coming here?"

"Exactly. Tell him never mind, that I've gone ahead to the club and to meet me there. Evil waits for no man and I can't have that maniac running all over New York. I've got to get to the bottom of this mystery."

Stockwell didn't speak another word. He ran off through the construction site and towards his destination.

The exterior of the Vagabond Club was nothing special. The entrance was a set of nondescript double doors at the top of a small flight of stairs. No doorman stood by. No canopy adorned the entrance. There was little but a small bronze plaque set beside door with the address to denote its presence in the greater city of New York.

It sat in the middle of a row of buildings that joined at their property lines. These neighbors dwarfed the single-story structure as they each rose up several stories above West 69th Street. All in all, the club looked like an unimportant building. Damian smiled. He liked it that way.

He strode up the steps, pushed open the double doors and stepped inside a small foyer. The room was empty save for one man sitting behind a counter.

"Good morning, Mister Stockwell." The clerk noted the torn nature of Stockwell's clothes. "It looks as if you've had a rough morning. Should I summon the tailor?"

"There's no time. Is Williams in?"

"He's just arrived."

Stockwell reached for the door and turned the handle. It would not turn.

"Unlock the door, my good man."

"Sir, I'm afraid I can't let you in without proper attire. You'll need a jacket to enter the club."

"But, I was forced to immolate mine in self-defense."

"I'm afraid those are the rules."

"I keep a spare in my quarters. Let me in and I'll don it."

"I'm sorry, sir. As you know, we have one available to loan."

Stockwell approached the desk. He stood to his full height and towered above the little man behind the desk. "You're new here, aren't you?"

"Yes, sir."

"You are aware of who I am?"

"Yes, sir, Mr. Stockwell. You're the man that needs to borrow a jacket."

"Open this door."

The little man behind the desk crossed his arms and leaned back in his chair.

Stockwell smiled and dove for the counter. Through scientific study and generous amounts of field research, he had proven conclusively that uppityness could be cured through a large dose of throttling. He always enjoyed the applied sciences.

He had not even reached the young man's throat when steel bars slammed down before him. The walls of the small foyer whirred and clanged as the oak veneer panels were pushed by hydraulic arms into a defensive position around the clerk.

Stockwell's hands grasped the steel. He glared at the clerk and shook the bars. They would not give. "Curse my inventive genius."

The clerk smiled from behind the safety of the cage. He leaned forward and pushed a switch on the desk. There was another whir from within the walls of the small room. A panel retracted and a mechanical arm extended holding out the loaner jacket.

Damian dropped his head, pulled it from the arm and put it on. It was far too small. It was tight across the back to such an extreme that he could not put his arms down for fear of rending the material.

There was a whir and a clack; the door to the club opened. Damian took a step toward the door then paused. Without turning, he addressed the clerk. "You're a good man, my boy. You've done your duty. I'll remember this."

With this said, Damian stepped through the door into the grand ballroom of the Vagabond Club. The floor gleamed. Mosaic artisans had spent months installing the separate tiles that formed the intricate pattern surrounding the club's crest in the center of the ballroom. Surrounding the crest's fierce eagle were the words vagus, calleo, recursus.

Stockwell uttered the phrase to himself, "To roam, to know, to return."

The atrium opened four stories above him to a series of skylights that sated the room in winter light. Each wall was covered in a mural that reached to the ceiling. And, each panel depicted a different scene from Greek mythology.

Icarus had always been his favorite. Even now, despite the awkward fit of the jacket, he stopped before it and admired the work. As it rose through the atrium, the mural portrayed Daedalus and his son's imprisonment on Crete, the construction of feather and wax into wings and their initial flight. Near the skylights, Icarus rose too close to the sun, despite his father's warnings, and the wax melted and he plummeted into the sea.

This tale of hubris spoke to the inventor in Stockwell and served as a reminder that despite his genius, his clever faculties and his inventive nature, no technology could ever master the forces of nature if it was made like crap. "Wax." He snorted. "Idiot." He focused on the image of Icarus flapping his arms. Stripped of their feathers, it was a useless gesture. Though futile, Damian admired the boy's gumption. Never give up. Never stop flapping.

Stockwell saluted the boy with a flap of his own arms.

The jacket ripped across the back.

"I can mend that for you." Williams's voice was always jovial.

Stockwell turned to greet him.

Before Damian could speak, Williams gasped at the mighty man's appearance.

"Dam, you're torn to shreds. What happened?"

"I picked a fight with a building."

"The building won, I see."

"We'll call it a tie." Stockwell had always found the club's outfitter pleasant and there was no man on earth better at his job. Should any member of the club need anything, Williams would find it and have it delivered anywhere on the planet. If it couldn't be found, Williams would design it and construct it.

"Come with me, Dam. I've got some thread in the shop."

"Don't mind the clothes, Williams. I'm here on an urgent matter."

"It must be if you don't mind looking like that. Walk with me to the shop and tell me what I can do for you."

The pair crossed the atrium to a set of double doors that led to the next building in the Vagabond Club complex. Though only the doughty foyer was labeled as such from the street, every building on the block comprised the clubhouse. In each building members could find all they needed to pursue adventure, exploration or relaxation.

Williams held the door as Stockwell passed into the club's dining room. The steak was world class and the menu constantly evolved as adventurers returned from their global excursions with exotic recipes that were gleefully given to the chef and shared with the other members. The Vagabond Club's kitchen was on the forefront of culinary excellence and would no doubt draw rave reviews from critics if it were open to the public. But the kitchen was open only to members and their guests.

"I hate to ask you into the shop, Dam, but we've been busier than usual and I can't afford to spend much time away."

"Why is that?"

Williams shrugged, "Hitler. No one knows what he's going to do. We've got people pushing up their plans to get ahead of the chaos or take advantage of it. Got my guys working around the clock prepping gear."

The couple continued through to the trophy room. The massive wood paneled room dwarfed Stockwell's personal collection. Animals and artifacts hung from the walls and resided within cases. There was no corner of the Earth or period in history that went unrepresented in the room.

They entered beneath a set of elephant tusks that crossed above the entrance and instantly felt the warmth from the fire in the massive hearth.

Williams waved his arm across the room, "See?"

Unlike the dining room, the trophy room was filled with members. It served not only as a museum but also as a communal room. Multiple seating areas drew the crowds here. Large upholstered chairs provided a comfortable place to converse; a place to share stories, some true, most embellished through retellings and whiskey—a large oak bar ran the entire length of the room. The furniture's comfortable construction made the room a perfect place to waste away hours in camaraderie. It also made it a popular room to grab a quick nap during research sessions.

Many members sat alone and poured over texts and documents, each searching or planning for their next expedition. Surrounded by the trophies of senior members, the juniors found inspiration in the setting. The established members found glory and often sat near their own contributions to the décor hoping to draw conversation from the younger hopefuls who had yet to put their skins on the wall.

Now every seat was filled. Charts that weren't being studied were being used to shield the light and allow for a moment's sleep.

Williams continued, "All the boats to Europe are about to be filled. I hope you're not heading that way."

"No. South, actually."

"I thought you hated the jungle."

Before Stockwell could answer, a small man covered in soot burst into the trophy room. His eyes darted around the room until he spotted Williams. He scrambled across the trophy room and almost tackled the man.

"Blast it, Roman. What's with you? And what have you done to your eyebrows?"

The little man felt at his forehead, adding more soot to his face. "There was a little accident with the bush cutter."

"What kind of accident?"

"It exploded. A little."

"Dam, I'm sorry. I've got to see to this."

"I understand. Go get some eyebrows on that guy. I'll wait here. Send for me as soon as things stop exploding. We need to talk."

Williams followed Roman back across the room, patting at embers that still smoldered on his coveralls as they went.

Stockwell checked his watch. Time wasn't something he could afford to waste but an explosion was an explosion. The upper floors of the building held apartments for out-of-town members. Damian kept one himself. Like the others in the room, he often found himself in a chair by the fire digging for clues in texts from the club's library. He rarely gave into sleep during these periods but found it convenient to have a bed nearby just in case.

There he kept a change of clothes. After a drink, he would change and hope that any fires the outfitter had to deal with were extinguished. The bartender saw him coming and placed his regular drink on the bar.

Damian lifted the rocks glass to his lips and was about to drink when he heard a fumbling at the Trophy Room's door. The doors shook but did not open. There was a banging and some muffled cursing from the other side. When the doors finally opened, Stockwell was delighted to see Bertrand enter.

He waved the Frenchman over and ordered a second drink for his valet.

"Good to see you, friend. What was with the door?"

Bertrand held up his bandaged hands. The gauze was fresh and rolled over itself several times to create a medicinal mitten. "The doorknob. It was difficult."

Stockwell chuckled. "Still. I'm glad you made it, my friend. After leaving you this morning, I was attacked by several men under the same ill effects of the mask that you wore. I'm still not sure what we're headed for, but it is certain to be a grand adventure."

The bartender set Bertrand's drink on the bar. Stockwell grabbed it and offered it to the Frenchman.

"Let's drink to adventure, Bertrand." Damian held out the drink and Bertrand closed his gauzed hands around it. Stockwell released it and reached for his own drink.

Unable to use his fingers, Bertrand's rocks glass slipped from his hands and broke on the floor.

Stockwell looked at the mess. "That's just sloppy, Bertrand."

The Frenchman hung his head.

Stockwell shot his whiskey and stood. "I'm going to change. Then we'll get to the bottom of this 'where Simmons went' nonsense."

He stepped away; Bertrand ordered another drink and requested a straw.

Stockwell and Bertrand entered the shop. The facility occupied the corner building in the Vagabond Club complex and still smelled like explosion. The shop was comprised of several vehicle bays and multiple workbenches in an open area. An office and an equipment room filled the remainder of the space.

Williams was yelling at several men dressed in coveralls as they scurried over the charred hulk of what Stockwell assumed was the bush cutter—no doubt another need based creation of the mechanical genius.

"Get these panels off and check the wiring. When that tank burst, it could have melted everything. Hurry up! This thing needs to be on a banana boat to Puerto Cortés in the morning."

"Williams."

The outfitter turned and smiled. He felt the fabric of Damian's fresh shirt. "Ah. You look much better now."

Damian pulled the mechanic's hands off his chest.

The mechanic smiled.

Damian let them go. "We need to talk."

Williams surveyed the work on the bush cutter and seemed satisfied that he could step away. "Of course. My apologies for the delay. One of our members is expecting this rig next week and explosions tend to ruin timetables." He waved them towards the office and offered each of them a coffee. They accepted and sat.

Damian sipped at his coffee. Bertrand fumbled the cup in his bandages and dropped it in his lap. He yelped in French and backed into a table. The bump knocked several papers from its surface. They scattered on the floor.

"Bertrand, please. We're guests here."

Williams handed Bertrand a shop rag. "What's with the golden gloves, Bertie?"

As Williams dabbed at the Frenchman's lap, Stockwell began to gather the files.

"Don't worry about him. We're looking for Simmons."

Williams shook his head, "Dam, you know I'd do anything to help you. But, you wrote the rules yourself. If a fellow Vagabond doesn't want to be found, I can't help you find him. Simmons asked that his position not be disclosed."

"I'm certain that was before he sent the distress call asking me to come to his assistance. Do you know where he is?"

"Of course. He's requested a great deal of equipment. But, I can't tell you."

"I understand the rules of the charter, Williams. But, this is a matter of life and death."

"Dam, you made me take an oath when I took this position. 'The praise and prize of each member's adventure is due to them alone. As is the risk they embrace.' You made me memorize it, remember?"

"Of course. And I admire that you are a man of your word. Now tell me where he is."

"If I shared his location with you, we'd be no better than the Explorers."

Damian chuckled and shook his head. "The Explorers, ha."

"Did you know they're still trying to get their silly little flag to Everest?"

Stockwell laughed heartily. "Won't they be surprised when they get there."

"How's that?"

"I wrote my name in the snow up there three years ago."

Williams laughed briefly then smiled, "I wish I could have seen that."

Stockwell shook off the amusement and continued to pick up the stack of papers. "Look, Williams, my friend is in danger. I know he's gone into the jungle—judging by the light in the transmission I'm assuming it was somewhere north of the equator. I'm not concerned about what he's after, I just need to find him."

The outfitter sighed and crossed his arms. His gaze wandered back to the shop as the workers began to strip the bush cutter's exterior panels.

Stockwell smiled, stood and placed the papers he had gathered back on the table. "Thank you, Williams. You've been a tremendous help."

"I didn't say anything."

"It was in what you didn't say that said what I needed to hear."

"What?"

Damian turned to Bertrand, "Call the hangar and have them fuel the Grumman for a flight to Puerto Cortés, Honduras."

Bertrand held up his bandaged hands.

Stockwell placed a pencil in the valet's mouth.

"Then call Cole Dalton at All-American Banana and tell him to expect us."

Bertrand left the shop after fumbling with the doorknob for a moment.

"It was that glance, wasn't it?" Williams stood and pointed to the vehicle bay outside the office window. "You knew the bush cutter was for Simmons?"

"Oh. Um ... no."

"Then how did you know about the banana company and Puerto Cortés?"

Stockwell picked up the top folder from the dropped stack. "It was in here. It says deliver to Peter Simmons, Puerto Cortés, Honduras. "

"And Cole Dalton?"

"Cole's an old friend. He now runs the AAB operation in Honduras. If anyone can help me find Simmons, it's him."

"Unbelievable."

"You held true to your oath, Williams. You're a good man. Even if you are a little sloppy with your files."

"Dam, you're amazing."

"I know."

# 11

## Face to Face

He didn't like the harbor. The ships rose too high. Their steel hulls formed caverns that closed in around him and choked out the ambient sounds of the city leaving only the grunts of the longshoremen and clanking of the hoists. It felt too distant from the rest of the world.

He moved quickly through the shipyard chasm and his eyes moved as quickly as his feet. They took in everything before and behind him, searching for an unseen foe that might use the setting to their advantage. Even with this cautiousness he moved with excitement. Witnessing Stockwell's fatal fall meant that he could finally return home and be done with this winter's cold.

Docked at the far end of the pier, the ship that had brought him to the cold and foreign land was preparing for departure. Crates hoisted by block and tackle swayed perilously overhead as they were loaded onto the deck of the ship. He didn't know what was in the crates. He didn't care. His only concern was the small berth that had been reserved for him for the voyage home.

The crew recognized him and did nothing to stop him from stepping onto the gangplank. His grip on the ropes that lined the walkway was solid and he moved quickly up the boards despite the presence of ice. He was eager to return to warmer climates, to the jungles. He stepped quickly but was stopped at the ship. A figure sat at the transom with his leg across the entrance. He did not look up when the assassin approached but focused instead on a small piece of wood in his hand that had been whittled into the shaped a small totem. His other hand held a large knife, generally considered too unwieldy for whittling. A wide-brimmed hat hid has face in shadow as he spoke.

"It is done?"

It was good to hear his native Spanish even if it was tainted with a foreigner's accent. He responded, "Yes, sir. It is done."

The man did not remove his leg. He pushed back in his chair and continued to shave details into the totem. "How did he die?"

"A fall from a great height. He defeated many men, but in the end it was the city that killed him."

"How many men?"

"Five. Including his own valet."

"I warned you not to underestimate him."

"I did not. But he was formidable beyond my estimation."

The man ceased carving and held the wood before his eyes. Unsatisfied, he placed the carving under the blade again. "That's kind of what underestimate means."

"How could anyone know of his abilities? His strength? It is beyond compare."

"I told you that he would not be easy to kill."

"He wasn't. But, he is dead."

The man dropped his leg and stood. On equal footing he would dwarf the assassin, but standing above him on the gangplank, his height was even more imposing. He set the totem down, but held the knife firmly in his hand.

"Is he?"

The assassin nodded with more than a little pride. He had killed the great Stockwell.

"No. He is not."

The news took from his face the color that the cold had not. He stammered his response, "How ... how? That's impossible."

"He trains for the impossible."

"I saw him die."

"You saw him fall. Others saw him walking into his precious social club."

"How could I know that he ..."

"The file I gave you should have prepared you for the impossible."

"Those stories could not have been true. I assumed they were myth. Legends dreamed by others. There is no way that those ..."

The man lifted the knife and the assassin began to sweat in the cold of air of New York Harbor.

"I ... I'll kill him, but I need more men. I need more masks."

"I gave you six."

"It wasn't enough. I placed them on strong men. They became stronger. But, he pulled the masks from their faces. He beat them soundly."

The man stepped forward.

The killer stepped back and lost his footing on a patch of ice. His grip on the ropes were all that prevented a plunge into the frigid waters. He fell to his knees. "Please. I will kill him! I just need more masks."

The man unbuttoned his pea coat and reached inside. "I only have one left."

He pulled out the mask and bent down to the groveling killer.

"No. No. Please."

The tall man placed the mask on the killer's face and the pleas ceased. The assassin stood, his lost balance corrected by the effects of the mask.

"Now. Are you going to kill Damian Stockwell?"

The man in the mask only nodded.

"Good. Step back on to the boat and let's go visit the engineer. We're going to make sure that mask doesn't come off."

# 12

## Dance of Death

The Duesenberg rolled wide around a corner and drifted into the oncoming lane. The honk of a horn sent it dodging back onto the right of the road. Traffic was thick with trucks that rumbled and rattled their cargo to destinations in the city from the warehouses that lined the street. There were few passenger cars in the district.

"Your driving is off today, Bertrand."

"Oui, Monsieur."

"Striking one of those trucks would put a quick end to our trip."

"The bandages do not make the wheel easy to hold, Monsieur."

"How long will you hide behind those wounds, Bertrand. It's unbecoming of you."

"It has been only today."

"Yes, but all day."

"Oui, Monsieur."

Brick warehouses lined the streets. Only the age of the bricks distinguished one building from the next. Even the company signs that hung from each were identical with only the printed names setting them apart. The names themselves were not dissimilar as each seemed to focus on shipping.

Stockwell watched as the placards passed: Universal Exports, Vel Verde Imports, Hidalgo Trading Company, Bengali Imports, Coronado Shipping. Each was the same. All but the final warehouse on the right.

It dwarfed the others and made its direct neighbor seem small in comparison. Even now the Hidalgo Trading Company sat in the shadow of DamIndustries. Not often given to fits of pride, Stockwell grinned proudly.

The Duesenberg stopped silently in front of the warehouse. After a few moments of fumbling, Bertrand pulled open the door and Stockwell stepped into the street. "Get the bags, Bertrand. I'll check in with Harrison."

The Frenchman nodded and moved to the trunk of the car where he continued to fumble with latches.

Stockwell had not reached the top step when the door was opened by a stocky man in a crisp blue uniform. His face did not match the fastidious nature of his clothes or the polish of his badge. In sharp contrast to his fancy uniform, Albie Harrison was extremely average.

"Good evening, sir."

"Harrison. How have you been? How's the family?"

"I don't have a family, sir."

"That's good to hear."

Harrison shook his head and stepped aside to let his employer in.

"Any action of late from next door?"

"Nothing from next door, but things have gotten pretty exciting around here."

"What kind of excitement?"

"I still can't believe it myself. A couple of nights ago, I was sitting in the office like I normally do when I heard a clicking."

"Like the drawing of a pistol's hammer?"

"No. There was lots of clicking. But all together...it's kind of hard to describe."

Stockwell nodded with interest. "I understand."

"At first I thought nothing of it. You know? It's just a clicking. Things click all the time. Hell, even sometimes my knee clicks when I get up too fast. But, the clicking, it keeps up and it keeps getting louder. I thought maybe it was one of the machines."

"So, I start looking around the warehouse to try and find the noise. I check the hangar, I check the lifts, I even looked in the hoods of all your cars. But, no clicking."

"And you're sure it wasn't coming from my antique bomb collection?"

"Oh, I'm sure, because when they tick I just run. I finally found where the clicking was coming from."

Stockwell rolled his eyes. "It wasn't the boiler again, was it? That thing just won't stay not broken."

"No, the boiler is fine. The clicking was coming from outside and it wasn't a clicking after all. It was a snapping."

"Like the breaking of a man's femur?"

"No. Like the snapping of a man's fingers. I looked outside and sure enough ..."

"Someone was snapping his fingers."

"No. There were lots of guys snapping their fingers. About fifty of them and all at the same time."

"Whoa, that's creepy."

"No. Well, yes, but it gets creepier."

"How?"

"Well, I said there about fifty guys, young guys—kids really—and half of them were up the street dressed in red and the other half were down the street dressed in white and they were walking down the street towards each with murder in their eyes."

"Murder?"

"Murder. There were eyeing each other up like they were going to rip each other's hearts out, take that heart home and then make a sandwich out of it or something and eat it."

"That's the look of murder for sure. I've seen it many times. They must have been running at each other and screaming with bloodlust."

"No. They were walking really slow like and not saying nothing. Just snapping."

Stockwell shivered. Evil took many forms in this world. At least if a killer was rushing you while screaming you knew it was safe to shoot them. This slow step approach was unnerving. Just hearing about made him hate the slow walking potential murderers.

"Really slow like. But what's stranger was they were walking together. Every stepped matched—all fifty of 'em. And they walked in step with the snaps. Every snap was a step. Just like this." Harrison backed away from Damian and hunched over. He snapped with each hand and slowly marched towards the adventurer. "Just like this. It was just like this."

"Harrison, that is disturbing. I hope you called the police."

"No. There was no time. Because they finally got close to each other."

"Was there bloodshed?"

"No. It was ... it was ..."

The security guard was struggling for words. What he had witnessed must have been horrific. Stockwell grabbed him by the shoulders and tried to shake the words from the man. "What happened, man? What did you see?"

"They finally met, right in front of the warehouse. Right in front of me and they pulled out knives like they were going to kill each other ... then they ... they danced."

"Danced? With each other?"

"No. Well, some of them did, but it was like them girls, the Rockettes. They all danced together but not like together, together.

They all moved the same way—spinning and twirling and all the time snapping."

"My God. You said some of them danced together?"

"No. I mean yes. They were the ones with the knives. They looked like they were trying to kill each other, but they were dancing so much that they couldn't stab each other right. And, if one came close, the other would jump back way out of the way and his buddies would catch him and then throw him back into the fight."

"It's horrific. At least they stopped snapping."

"No. They kept snapping. The whole time snapping." Harrison paused—lost in the horror of that night. "Sometimes, when I close my eyes, I can still hear the snapping."

"Harrison?" The guard was no longer speaking to him.

"And that snapping is coming for me. It's the snapping of fifty men. And they all want to dance with me."

Stockwell never liked to yell at his employees, it hurt his throat, but this called for drastic action. "Harrison!"

The guard snapped from his waking nightmare and looked at his boss. The man looked a little confused as if he had just returned suddenly to place that was unfamiliar to him.

"Yeah, boss?"

"What happened next? After the dancing and knives and the ... knife dancing?"

"Oh, I shot at them."

"You shot at them?"

"Well, I didn't have a hose to turn on them, sir."

"Harrison, you can't just go shooting at kids!"

"Why not?"

"Well, you make a good point there. Was anyone hurt?"

"No, they scattered after a couple of warning shots and I doubt they'll be back."

"Why do you say that?"

"After I shot at them, I yelled, 'and don't come back.'"

"That's a solid plan. Good work, Harrison."

"Thank you, sir."

"Is the Goose ready?"

"Yes, sir. Bertrand called and I've got her all fueled up."

"You're a good man, Harrison. Do me a favor and help Bertrand with the luggage. He's been whining about his hands all day."

"Yes, sir."

Harrison left the office as Stockwell paged through the daily reports. Aside from the notation that the Goose had been fueled and the dance/stabbing had been foiled, there was little of note in the ledger. The only other entry marked the delivery of a package that was being kept in the office safe.

Stockwell crossed the Spartan office to the large Mosler safe. He had made it a point early on to never learn a safe's combination. Instead of memory, he relied on sensitive fingers to feel the tumblers align. Without watching, he spun the dial left, stopped and spun in back to the right. A third spin of the dial and twist of the handle opened the safe door. It was the second package he had received that day in a nondescript brown paper wrapping.

The first had led to his attempted murder at the hands and feet of his friend and set the duo on a course that put many lives in peril. The second could easily do the same.

Without a sound, the Mosler's door opened. The package had been dropped on the top shelf without caution. Damian carefully removed the package. After having seen the assassin's weapon in action at the construction site, he envisioned a clever postal bomb that would disintegrate the recipient like the stacks of bricks.

He examined the address label and his concerns vanished as he tore at the paper. A smile grew on his face as the paper fell away to reveal a box marked as originating from the Smith & Wesson Performance Center. A close friend in the center often asked Stockwell to field test new innovations and he was always eager to oblige.

Inside the box was a note:

Dam,

I know how you're fond of warnings shots. Thought you might like to give this a try. It holds eight rounds of .357. That's seven warnings and one I told you so. Please let us know how it performs.

-Carl

The revolver was massive and the metal was raw. This suited Damian's immediate needs perfectly. Often the high shine found on many of his firearms served to unnerve his enemies. With this bizarre mask situation, however, Stockwell preferred that the first light they see come from the muzzle flash.

He tucked the revolver into his waistband and moved into the hangar as Harrison and Bertrand dragged the luggage in the doorway.

The cavernous warehouse served as a launch point for all his adventures. As such, it was equipped with everything needed to battle evil no matter where it should occur. Several vehicles lined the eastern wall. Custom built motorcycles, heavily tuned cars and reinforced trucks, each sat before a door that led to the streets of New York. He moved past these to a staircase that led up to a series of catwalks suspended from the ceiling. This system of walkways allowed him to cross over the Hudson River which filled the center of the warehouse. Docked along the channel were several boats and the Grumman Goose that would take him to Honduras. The floatplane's range and landing flexibility made it the ideal adventurer's plane. But, he also thought the machine beautiful and elegant. It sat at the ready for him to call upon her when needed. He treated her with delicate care and a soft touch, but she could be pushed to the extreme and ridden hard when he demanded. He had christened the aircraft the *Dahlia*. It could also be loaded from the rear.

Admiring the plane from above, he crossed over the catwalk and descended to the far side of the warehouse. Chain-link fences formed several storage cages along the western wall and he made his way to the largest one and opened the door.

Wooden chests lined the cage. Damian opened the cabinet doors to one and revealed a series of drawers. Each was labeled with a caliber and he quickly found the .357 drawer and pulled it open. Every round had been made to his specifications by the same man that sent him the new revolver. He pulled out several boxes and shut the door.

The round had stopping power; that was undeniable. However, this was the first time that he knew a weapon would do him little good. All but one of the men that had tried to kill him today wore a mask that had robbed them of their humanity. Those that wore the mask could not be blamed, and therefore shot, because of their actions. His instinct told him that he had not seen the last of the horrific mask.

For a moment he considered placing the weapon aside but his instinct also told him to be prepared. And, even though they were now at odds, his instincts were never wrong.

Another cabinet revealed a selection of holsters and gun belts. After trying several pistol holsters and finding each a poor match for the large revolver, he pulled a rifle scabbard from another cabinet and took it to a workbench. The pistol was almost half the length of a rifle and within a matter of moments he had worked the leather scabbard into a form-fitting holster for the test weapon. He dropped this and the ammo boxes into a canvas duffle bag and left the cage.

As he moved along the edge of the dock, he inspected the exterior of the *Dahlia*. He smiled. She had been through rough weather and several firefights, but the old girl always kept her figure.

Bertrand had boarded on the far side of the plane and began stowing luggage. Stockwell carried the canvas duffle to the cockpit and began his preflight check. The Frenchman joined him and took the copilot's seat.

"Are you ready, Bertrand?"

Bertrand nodded.

"Then, it's off to adventure." Stockwell turned the engines over as the remotely controlled hangar doors began to open. "It's a long flight, my friend. But I'm kind of looking forward to no one trying to kill me for a while."

That's when the man in the boat opened fire with a machine gun.

# 13

## Red Rockets Glare

Bullets slammed against the *Dahlia's* hull in rapid succession. The large caliber slugs marred the thick windshield and sparked as they struck the skin of the cockpit. Stockwell and Bertrand sat calmly as the muzzle of the assassin's Thompson automatic flashed repeatedly.

Bullets scarred the windshield with deep crevices but the panel did not shatter. All of the glass in the plane was comprised of Damite, a specially formulated polymer that retained the transparency and weight of glass but adopted the strength and resiliency of steel.

Between muzzle flashes, Damian could see that the man's face was hidden by the horrid expression of one of the masks. This did not surprise him but it did disappoint him. The reaction on a gunman's face when they first encountered Damite was something he always enjoyed.

Robbed of this pleasure, Stockwell grab the throttles and shoved them forward to the stops. The *Dahlia's* engines roared as fuel and air rushed together to explode in a barely contained rage. Deafening noise filled the hangar. Flames spit from the exhausts like anger from the snout of a mad bull. The props spun with furious abandon and the blast from their motion blew back into the hangar. Cages rattled, papers fluttered and the plane began to creep slowly forward into the Hudson.

The gunman reloaded and emptied another magazine into the skin of the plane before suffering a jam in the drum. Stockwell smiled as the nose of the plane emerged from the hangar.

"What is it you are doing?"

"Bertrand, we're going to run over that boat."

"What if he is an innocent man?"

"The gun is new and the mask is new, but it's more than the face and weapon that make the man. His posture. His poise when firing. This is the assassin from the construction yard returned to finish what he tried to start back there at the yard."

Bertrand shook the confusing statement from his mind. "What if you're wrong?"

"Wrong? Ha. I'm willing to bet his life on it."

The *Dahlia* cleared the hangar and Stockwell began to turn the craft. He stood and removed his thick winter coat. Its down would restrict his movements. The leather sling containing the Smith & Wesson went across his back.

"Take the wheel, Bertrand, and cripple his vessel."

Bertrand held up his bandaged hands.

Stockwell smiled back and held up his fist. "That's right, my French friend. Dukes up. It's time to show this cad that evil will get him nowhere."

Bertrand sighed and tried to grip the yoke with the gauze mittens. "He is getting away."

Stockwell looked back out the windshield. The wooden sport boat had throttled up its own engine and was moving quickly into the river.

The *Dahlia* cut through the boat's wake. Its deep hull design was rated in seas up to five feet—the wake was barely noticeable. Bertrand worked the rudder with his feet and finished the turn by pulling in behind the boat.

"We've got him now. He won't be able to outrun us for long." Stockwell dug into a supply bin and pulled out a length of rope. "Take out his craft and I'll pull him from the water."

"He's coming back."

Stockwell turned back to the cockpit. The wooden sport boat had indeed turned and was heading back towards the plane. Damian could see the muzzle flash of the Thompson but the boat was well out of effective range.

"What is he doing?" Bertrand continued to wrestle with the yoke as the plane accelerated.

"He means to ram us."

"Like we were trying to ram him. Good."

"True, but a head-on collision could cripple the *Dahlia* as well. This would prevent our departure. Go faster, Bertrand."

"We cannot." Bertrand nodded to the throttles.

The *Dahlia* was not far from gaining lift, but it would be close.

As the two vehicles drew closer in proximity, bullets began to once again splash off the hull and windscreen.

"C'mon, Bertrand." Stockwell leaned on the throttles as the Frenchman pulled back on the stick. The plane began to bounce as Bernoulli's principle began to take effect.

The boat sped closer.

The *Dahlia's* nose lifted and dropped back into the Hudson. The resulting splash took some of the much needed momentum.

The boat was less than a hundred yards away. At full speed it would surely damage the hull of the amphibian.

"Zut alors. We will not make it in time." Bertrand's bandaged hand slipped from the flight yoke. The resulting action drove the left pontoon into the water. Stockwell was almost thrown from his feet. More drag. Less speed. They were almost out of options.

"We have one last chance. Let's just hope Dr. Goddard's device works."

Stockwell grabbed the captain seat and steadied himself. He reached above his head and flipped a switch. A hum from the back of the plane signaled that the cargo ramp was lowering.

"Frenchman, grab that stick!"

Bertrand grabbed the yoke.

The boat was 150 yards away.

"And don't forget to jettison the rockets because there's a pretty good chance they might explode." Stockwell hit two more switches. There was a whine and then a fwoosh as two liquid fueled rockets, one beneath each wing, erupted in to a burst of flame and acceleration.

Bertrand was thrown back into his seat as the *Dahlia* plowed through the river casting huge plumes of water into the air. He fought to hold on to the yoke and pull it back to his chest.

Stockwell was running. The paragon of fitness dashed through the cabin, his mighty legs driven by trained muscles and a desire for justice.

The boat was upon them. Bertrand forced more give from the yoke than he thought possible and the nose began to rise. The rocket propelled plane broke from gravity's feeble grip and took to the air as the sport boat raced under the v-shaped hull.

The pitch of the plane drove Stockwell faster to the *Dahlia's* tail. He placed one final step on the cargo ramp and propelled himself into the air. He hung for a moment between the plane and the river before gravity took hold and pulled him towards the frigid winter waters of the Hudson.

Time slowed. He knew it to be a trick of the mind. Adrenaline coursed through his system. Nerves fired faster and the world around him crawled. He looked down and saw the wake of the plane rushing forward. He tucked and rolled in midair. In the middle of his acrobatic maneuver he saw the boat enter his vision.

Despite the rush of prop wash and the wake of the *Dahlia*, the gunman had not lost his balance. His hands were still on the wheel of the craft and he was in control of the boat. The dead eyes of the mask, however, were turned toward the plane that he had failed to strike.

Damian completed the summersault in midair and aimed his feet like a weapon before driving like a cast stone into the man's chest.

The gunman fell to the right as Stockwell collapsed to the rear deck of the wooden craft. The assassin had kept his grip on the wheel and the fall resulted in a violent turn that took the pair into the wake of the plane.

The boat leapt from the water and landed on its side, perilously close to capsizing.

Stockwell dropped toward the water, only to be caught by the gunwale.

The assassin released the wheel and the boat turned violently back to the right. Stockwell rolled to his feet in time to block the butt of the Thompson as it soared toward his head.

The assassin responded with a knee to Damian's solar plexus and doubled the titan over. A haymaker landed on the back of his neck and drove him back on the decking of the boat.

Bertrand had not been fully prepared for the sudden takeoff provided by the rockets. His grip on the yoke had been tenuous before and only by wrapping his arms around the stick had he been able to lift off. Now, the *Dahlia* was moving faster than he could ever remember.

Beneath the wings, the rockets continued to burn, adding thrust to the flight. Bertrand wasn't sure if the props were even contributing to the forward motion. Damian and Goddard's system had never been tried before. In fact, the rocket scientist had tried to talk Damian out of it saying it was "too dangerous," "an unnecessary risk" and "something only an idiot would even considering doing."

Damian had insisted and now Bertrand was behind the wheel of the first rocket powered Goose in history. The honor aside, Bertrand was terrified as the fuselage shook around him. Grumman had not designed the craft for this. They couldn't have. This didn't really exist.

The liquid fueled rockets drove the Goose into the sky at an angle the Frenchman didn't think was possible. He had to level it out and release the rockets before they overheated. He pushed against the yoke, trying to force the nose down. Now the rocket's thrust fought against him.

Every muscle in his abdomen strained as he fought to lean up from the seat. Bertrand grimaced as the stick crept toward the dash and the *Dahlia's* nose slowly began to level out. It was several moments before gravity was pulling at his feet instead of his back. Once free from the mighty grip, Bertrand was able to gain control of the craft.

He checked his position and was surprised to find how far the rockets had taken him from the boat. And where was Damian? He had last seen his employer running towards the rear of the plane.

Bertrand turned to look for him. The cargo door was down. Had he fallen out?

The plane still groaned from the force of the rockets, but it responded when Bertrand coaxed it into a wide right bank over the island of Manhattan.

Out the window, he saw the boat that tried to ram them moments before. It was wildly out of control.

Bertrand had known Stockwell long enough to understand what had happened. Somehow, Damian had gotten on the boat and was no doubt the reason it was out of control.

He pushed the plane harder into the turn. The airframe protested with groans and squeaks. The rockets were a burden now but would be a blessing as soon as he was able to straighten out ... if the *Dahlia* held together.

The Grumman Goose was all but perpendicular to the ground and Bertrand looked through the copilot's window to the streets below. What a site he must have been to the people in Manhattan—a silver banshee screaming flames above the skyscrapers.

Despite the beating she was taking, the *Dahlia* held together and leveled out on course with speeding boat below. So desperate to climb moments before, Bertrand now pointed the nose back at the water, hoping to get close enough to the boat to help his employer.

Cityscape quickly changed to water as the *Dahlia* roared back over the river. Bertrand's focus was single-minded until he heard the buzzing. Even then, he ignored it. The alarm, no doubt, was caused by the toll the rockets were putting on the airframe. There was nothing he could do about that now.

It was only a moment later that Bertrand remembered what Stockwell said about the rockets exploding. He quickly engaged the autopilot and searched for the rocket engine release switches. He found them above his head next to a flashing red light that was labeled, "explode."

Bertrand reached up to hit the switch. The gauze enshrouding his hands prevented him from doing anything but mashing the control panel. The buzzing came faster. Bertrand mashed. He mashed the panel harder and accomplished nothing.

The buzzing was near constant. The Frenchman screamed and brought his foot over his head. It connected with the panel.

Teak met face as the haymaker drove Stockwell to the deck of the boat. He rolled quickly as the Thompson began to chatter. His leg drove the barrel of the gun up into the air and sent the masked assassin back into the cockpit of the craft.

The boat veered right and Damian used the momentum to get back to his feet. He rushed the gunman, grabbed the weapon and drove it against the would-be killer's chest. Stockwell stepped in closer, restricting the gun's movements.

The assassin launched out with knees and elbows as the two men struggled for control of the submachine gun.

Stockwell absorbed these strikes and fought back with his own, kicking at the man's instep and knees. He glared into the soulless eyes of the mask and cursed its effects. This coward was smaller than he and weaker, no doubt, without the aid of the mask. What was its secret? How could it affect a man's nerves and muscles as it did?

He had to get a hold of one without it self-destructing.

Stockwell scored a knee to the masked-man's ribs. The force doubled his opponent over and twisted the Thompson free with such force that the weapon flew overboard and splashed into the river.

The grim expression on the mask lurched forward and drove itself into Stockwell's face. It hit like a 2 x 4. The massive man stumbled back. There was a roaring in his ears. Had he been struck so hard?

The roaring grew louder and he realized that it wasn't in his head. He turned to see the arrival of the *Dahlia* just as the rockets released from the plane.

"Bertrand!" Stockwell screamed and dropped to the floor of the boat as the rockets slammed into the water on either side of the craft. The *Dahlia* screamed overhead as the remaining fuel in the rockets exploded.

Geysers of river water erupted forty feet in the air and the boat was blown from the water. Stockwell could hear the wooden hull cracking from the blast as it was lifted from the river and threatened to turn stern over bow.

The boat was now vertical and Damian was rolled forward. His massive frame hit the seats and stopped. At this speed, if the boat flipped, it was sure to strike him. The resulting blow would, at best, render him unconscious and drifting in the frigid waters of the Hudson.

The bow hit the water first. The tip of the boat dragged a channel in the water. If more of it caught, the resistance would flip the craft.

Stockwell grabbed on to the seat hoping to maintain his grip if the craft should turn on him.

The bow skimmed across the water for what seemed minutes before the weight of the outboard pulled the stern back into the water. Timbers sheared from the boat as the blasted planks tore away. The boat slowed as it took on water. Though the engine still drove it forward, it began to wobble due to the hull's fractured integrity.

It was difficult to stand. The craft lurched from side to side and grew more violent with each moment. Stockwell had finally pulled himself to his feet when the boat struck Liberty Island.

# 14

## Inside Lady Liberty

Amid a thousand splinters and the bursting snaps of wooden planks, Damian Stockwell soared through the air. He had always savored the sweet taste of liberty. His moral code was more or less built around the idea that all men should be free to pursue their own desires unfettered by the shackles of man or nations. But, Liberty Island tasted like dirt. He landed hard at the base of a retaining wall in a pile of loose soil.

He spit the taste of liberty from his mouth and stood ready to defend himself from the assassin. If he could recover so quickly from such a remarkable wreck, he had no doubt that the mask's effect on the man's nervous system would enable him to recover even quicker.

No attack came. Perhaps the crash had shaken free the mask's mysterious hold. The man would still be dangerous, but without the heightened senses and added strength, he would be easier to take down.

The bank of the island was small and there was no place for the killer to hide. Where had he gone? Had the scoundrel even cleared the boat? Or was his villainous body still trapped in the heap?

Stockwell inched back towards the wreckage, his incredible imagination moving ahead of time. He pictured the assassin, still bearing the mask, bursting from the crashed sport boat with vicious silence to continue the assault. Damian had faced all manner of horrors in the course of his adventures: man at his darkest, creatures at their most mysterious, beasts in their most rabid states—he was afraid of nothing. But when things jumped out from out of nowhere, it kind of made him jump a little. Sometimes he shrieked, but it was a manly shriek of surprise and not fear. He stepped back away from the wreckage and wondered if there was a stick somewhere around that he could use to poke it with.

A scream of terror came from Lady Liberty's platform. Several more followed and it was clear that the masked assassin was not in the boat but that he had fled into the park and was terrifying the innocents that wanted nothing more than to pay their respects to the lovely lady.

Damian sighed and turned away from the boat. Several quick steps and a mighty leap took him up the retaining wall and into the park. Liberty Enlightening the World rose above him, her patina skin a beacon for the denizens of the world that sought freedom from oppression, hunger, tyranny and colder climates. Every time he saw the glorious woman, his heart swelled with pride that the world was as attracted to her as he was.

But, now people scattered from her. They ran in horror from the pedestal that held her up for the world to see. Frightened citizens cowered in her shadow behind benches and trash receptacles. They fled from the statue's entrance with screams that pierced his very patriotism. This could not be happening.

As others ran from Lady Liberty, Stockwell dashed through the plaza and into the visitor's center. The crowd had thinned but screams persisted. He rushed to the observation deck elevator. The doors were closing but he saw inside the hideous mask and several frightened visitors being held at gunpoint.

"You cad!" Stockwell's voice boomed in the small foyer.

The man in the mask turned the weapon on Stockwell. The Thompson had been lost to the water and Damian wished he was facing down the barrel of the .45 automatic instead. The strange weapon from the construction site was in the assassin's hand. He pulled the trigger.

Damian rolled out of the way as a stream a green liquid shot from the elevator and into the lobby. His actions took him out of the way but the green liquid landed on a replica of the statue's face. The left side of her face dissolved.

Names, slurs and insults came rushing forth to Stockwell's tongue. The rage he felt was unlike anything he had experienced before. He turned back to the elevator to let this coward have it, but the doors had closed and its ascent had begun.

Stockwell rushed across the lobby and slammed into the doors. Though he knew it was futile, he beat his fists against the steel. The car behind them was gone.

He eyed the entrance to the stairs but did not take them. Even at peak condition he knew that he could not beat the elevator to the top and today he had already crashed a boat, jumped from a plane, been shot at, been dropped from a building and kicked a lot of ass.

There was still one last ass left to kick and he would need every ounce of strength he had left. Stockwell sat. A bench in the lobby made for a comfortable perch with a clear line of sight to the elevator door.

Long ago he had learned to never waste a moment. Time was about the only thing he could not buy more of and it angered him when he found himself throwing it away on wasted actions.

Forced to wait for an elevator's return so that he could pursue a possessed killer to the top of the Statue of Liberty was precisely the kind of time that should not be squandered.

Often he used moments between gunfights to put his mind against problems he sought to solve in the lab. World hunger, medical breakthroughs, whiter whites—his endeavors were numerous and, more times than not, the epiphanies arrived in these unrelated times. It was crucial, he believed, to step away from a problem to better understand it.

In this particular case he would use the time to clear his mind of his rage. If directed, it could be a powerful ally but that was not how anger worked. Anger was a liability in the fight against evil. One's own rage conspired with the enemy against him. The assault on the public and Lady Liberty's face had tapped into that anger and released it upon him.

Tibetan monks had instructed him in the art of meditation. Introspective thinking mixed with rhythmic breathing often led to a clearer mind. The monks had told him that it aligned his spirit with the world and brought all things in to balance. Though he had proven all of the techniques to be scientific in nature, the public still looked upon the practice as spiritual mysticism, so when discussing the practice he simply referred to it as Damian's Thinky Time.

He closed his eyes and took several deep breaths. The anger faded. Then it came back and he got angry but it quickly faded again. He turned his now calm mind to the situation at hand.

The last few actions of the madman had taken him by surprise. Withdrawing into the statue was out of character for the masked killers. They had always attacked, never retreated. Even this crazed killer had tried to ram the *Dahlia*, which would have meant death for himself. There was only one answer to this puzzle. The assassin knew what his target had already survived and that there was no way to beat him on level ground. The killer would use the confines of the statue and possibly the statue's height itself to try and kill the famed adventurer. The assassin would be done running now. He would be lying in ambush.

The elevator rose to shoulder level of the great statue. From there one could descend back to the ground via a system of stairs or ascend to the observation level at the crown. A third possible avenue existed up the statue's outstretched arm to the torch. Damian had been to the crown many times but never to the torch. That section had been closed for more than twenty years—ever since a cowardly saboteur had detonated an arms warehouse on the neighboring Black Tom Island. The resulting explosion had thrown debris and shrapnel into the city and the statue. Lady Liberty's robe has absorbed a great deal of it with little concern. But the shoulder had been impacted in such away that it threatened to fall. Since that day, visitors had not been allowed to view the world as lit by the torch of freedom.

Regardless, the doors would open at only one point and he would be an easy target for the waiting gunman. There was no way to access the elevator shaft. All he could do was board the car and wait for the trap to spring. But, he had a plan.

He reached over his shoulder and pulled the large revolver from the sling. He smiled. It was important to have a plan.

The one draw back to Damian's Thinky Time was that he often lost track of time. This time was no different. The elevator chimed its arrival. The doors slid open and Stockwell's rage returned.

On the floor of the car were several bodies. Parts of each had been melted away by the devious device of the masked gunman. Vapors still rose from the victims as Stockwell stepped inside and adjusted the controls that would take him into the trap.

# 15

## Head and Shoulders

Stockwell took refuge in the corner of the elevator as the doors opened. He expected a stream of green acid to jet into the car the moment it arrived but there was none. He stepped onto the metal flooring of the statue's shoulders. The area was empty. Ahead lay the staircase to the observation deck. It spiraled up into the statue's face and led to the crown. Those with a fear of height or claustrophobia would find its design overwhelming.

Wind blew against the skin of the statue and transferred the sound to the interior. The dull roar made it difficult to hear anything, but over the din he recognized the sound of weeping. It was coming from the crown.

Fear for his own safety was never a part of his plans; even now he knew that there were people in need of his aid. He bounded up the spiral stair at such a speed that he was fighting not only gravity, but centrifugal force as well. The low railing would do little to keep him on the staircase should he lose his balance. And, beyond the rail was a straight drop to the feet of liberty.

He was ten feet from the crown when the coward revealed himself. The masked killer stood at the foot of the stairs that led to the torch.

Stockwell condemned the man for his actions. "You're not supposed to be there. That section is closed to public access."

The stream of acid struck the railing and Stockwell's handhold evaporated. His massive frame rolled over the side of the stairs. He plummeted ten feet before grabbing the rail of a lower flight. The grip was solid but there was no telling how long before another jet of acid would take it from him.

The bulk of the stairwell separated him from his attacker and the assassin fired blindly. Kachunks preceded each blast and they began to come quicker. The green acid struck everywhere. It slowly ate away at the staircase but also contacted several of the girders that supported the statue itself. Green mist began to fill the area. Stockwell had to put a stop to this.

There was no clear shot. He held the massive revolver in his hand but could not find the killer in its sights. More green ooze struck more of the copper skin and daylight began to appear inside the statue. He had to do something, but what?

The gong. During his fight with Bertrand, the banging of the gong has disrupted the mask's influence momentarily. Stockwell surveyed the area. There was nothing but steel and copper.

He felt the staircase shift. The acid had eaten away at enough of the supports that it was about to collapse. There was no gong in the statue so he would be forced to settle for the next best thing.

Stockwell raised his .357 and fired a round in the back of the statue's face.

The resulting boom was thunderous. The report bounced off the copper skin and multiplied. The clang of the shell added to the cacophony and created a ring that even Stockwell felt.

He pulled himself back on the staircase. Though he was gripping his ears, the villain was quickly regaining his composure.

Stockwell fired again and again the assassin writhed in pain and grabbed at his ears. Damian rushed back down the stair firing a new shot every time the killer pulled his hands away from his ears. The killer struggled to climb the stairs to the torch and managed to scramble ahead of Stockwell's line of fire.

Damian reached the lower platform and ran to the base of the stairs. The assassin was waiting at the top with the devious weapon pointed at Stockwell's feet. The kachunk told Damian to leap out of the way but the assassin was a step ahead. The green liquid landed at Stockwell's feet and spread in a puddle. Damian fired the eighth and final shot from his .357 as the floor beneath him fell away. He dropped.

He caught himself on the newly formed hole. The residue of the acid burned through his shirt and ate at his skin. His feet dangled out the armpit of the glorious statue.

His final shot, thrown off by the drop, had struck the canister on the strange weapon. It erupted and sprayed its contents on the side of Lady Liberty's wrist. Daylight poured into the narrow passageway.

The assassin opened the door at the top of the stairway and ran to the torch.

Stockwell grit his teeth as he tried to ignore the acid burns and lifted himself back into the statue. He slid the empty gun back in its sling and surveyed the damage. The Statue of Liberty had been ruined, defiled by the crazed madman who had left himself nowhere to run.

He needed the assassin alive. He had questions he needed answered, but it was going to kill him not to kill him. Stockwell stomped up the stairs. The noise echoed with every step he took. He was no longer trying to disrupt the mask's effect. He just wanted the villain to know he was coming.

Damian Stockwell burst through the door and the killer was upon him.

He landed on Stockwell's back and locked an arm under the goliath's chin. Stockwell rolled forward and tumbled the assassin onto the platform. He had reversed the hold and now had the killer by the throat.

"I want answers, you fiend. And, I'm going to get them." Stockwell grabbed the edge of the mask and pulled. It didn't give. He gave several tugs and it remained in place. Stockwell examined the mask trying to see what held it firm. The others had been difficult to remove but this one was impossible. That's when he saw it. This one was different. Several bolt heads protruded from the surface of the mask.

Stockwell looked at his hand. His palm was covered in blood. Someone had bolted the mask to the killer's face.

"My God. What evil have I encountered."

The killer took advantage of Stockwell's distraction and leapt to his feet. Stockwell dropped into a defensive stance. The wind itself was an opponent at this height. Gusts threatened to blow both of the men from their feet. The platform was sturdy, but the railing had not been maintained since the observation deck had been closed. It was a perilous setting with a ruthless opponent. Stockwell smiled. The fight was on.

A flurry of fists struck for Damian's head but this man had not had the training of his valet. The punches were fierce but unskilled. Stockwell's Damitsu blocked and provided a counterstrike for every punch thrown. He was merciless and with each blow he made sure the cad knew why he was beating him.

The first blow put the killer on his heels. "You've murdered the innocent."

Another sent his head crashing into the torch. "You've violated Lady Liberty with your spray."

Stockwell caught a punch and pulled the killer in close. "And, you made me shoot Liberty in the face."

The killer dove forward and tried to drive the mask into Damian's face. Stockwell stepped to one side and caught the man by the hair. He spun and drove the man into the torch mask first. The hideous face ruptured. Green mist began to seep from the eyes and mouth of the horrid expression. The horrible face began to dissolve and the assassin began to scream.

The pain must have been unbearable. The corrosive gas that was designed to consume the mask had nowhere to go and rushed over the man's face.

Stockwell backed up as the killer grasped at the mask. Somewhere between the strike and now, he had regained conscious thought.

The mask disappeared and what was left was inhuman. Melted skin boiled and puss ran from blisters and obscured the killer's eyes. Bloody metal bolts protruded from what was the man's face. He continued to scream and began to flail. Stockwell reached to stop him but in his pain the killer backed too close to the edge and fell from the torch of Liberty Enlightening the World.

Damian rushed to the edge and watched the man fall. Shortly before he struck the ground he became fully aware of his situation. Stockwell could see it in what used to be the man's face.

# 16

## Out of Town on a Rail

The long flight to Puerto Cortés was spent, in part, coordinating the repair efforts of the statue. Lady Liberty would have to be closed to the public for the better part of a year. Though it disheartened Stockwell to deny her beauty to the common man, it was more important that her promise live on for future generations and that her blazing torch of freedom would light the world's way for years to come.

The battle inside her robe had put the glorious girl in jeopardy. The chemical from the assassin's weapon had weakened the infrastructure in several places. Parts of her skin had been burned through completely. The arm that bore the torch threatened to collapse. She stood more now out of principle than of girders.

Upon reaching the ground, Stockwell had rushed into action and made several calls to branches of DamIndustries. Within an hour, construction crews had arrived to stabilize the statue. From the Dahlia's radio telephone he continued to arrange her repair. Locating and processing copper and iron was only a matter of coordinating the proper factories, though he called several clients personally to let them know that their orders had taken a backseat to freedom.

Damian set the phone on the receiver, took his place in the pilot's seat and sighed.

"It is done?" Bertrand had dutifully watched the instruments while his employer was on the phone.

"Yes. I've called Tombstone and the funding is arranged. The factories will be running double shifts for the foreseeable future, but Lady Liberty will be stronger than ever."

"It is quite commendable, Monsieur, that you would do such a thing."

"A man must pay for his mistakes, Bertrand."

"But it was not your fault."

"Of course it was. If not for me, he would never have crashed on the island."

"But, you could not have known."

Stockwell stared into the night ahead of them. The thrum of the engines was calming to him. Their constant buzz meant progress. Few things frustrated him more than sitting still; especially when a friend's life was in peril. The mighty adventurer shook his head. "It doesn't matter. She stands for everything great in this world, my French friend. This you should know as she was a gift from your nation to ours for being so amazing. I cannot let a symbol as powerful as her become endangered."

Bertrand's eyes returned to the dials for a moment then back to his employer, "Monsieur, the cost must be enormous."

Stockwell shrugged and turned his eyes back to his copilot. "Wealth is just another benefit of being raised in a pitchblende mine. It afforded me great strength and great wealth. Not everyone can be so fortunate. It's my duty to give all of my blessings to the world."

"Perhaps now I could ask for a raise?"

Stockwell laughed and stood from his seat. He put his hand on Bertrand's shoulder. "You're a good friend, Bertrand. You know just how to make me laugh. You and I are too alike; we live for the adventure, the thrill. Money means nothing to us. I'm going to get some rest. Let me know when we reach Puerto Cortés. It'll be good to see Dalton again. It's been too long. Maybe he can help us crack the mystery of Simmons's disappearance."

"Oui, Monsieur."

"Good night, my friend. Until tomorrow when the adventure continues."

The Dahlia lay down easy in the calm waters of Puerto Cortés. Her buoyant pontoons nestled gently into the waves and she rolled calmly to the dock.

Bertrand had roused Stockwell from a peaceful sleep half an hour outside of the coastal city. Damian had quickly performed a morning routine of stretching and calisthenics that were designed to invigorate and awaken his muscles, his mind and all five of his senses. Once the routine was complete, he took the yoke and set the plane down in the harbor.

Bertrand moved sluggishly to the hatch when instructed to toss the shore man a line, but the Frenchman complied. Bertrand had flown through the night, or more precisely, allowed the plane's autopilot to fly through the night. The valet struggled with the door and the mooring line but managed to toss an end to the harbor crew.

Gruff Hondurans pulled the Dahlia fast to dock and the two men disembarked. Stockwell's powerful frame filled the plane's doorway as he looked out into the city. The port city was almost four hundred years old but little of the original colonial buildings were visible. Fruit storehouses, housing mostly bananas, obscured any view beyond the docks. The town had exploded over the last thirty years thanks to the influx of American investment. The fruit companies had modernized the port and brought transportation to the Central American nation in the form of extensive rail lines. These lines plunged into the city delivering the lifeline of commerce.

It was for this reason Stockwell had called upon his old friend Cole Dalton. As the local head of one of the major fruit growers, he had access to the trains. And Stockwell needed to move inland fast.

Stockwell and Dalton also shared a history with Simmons. If Peter was indeed in Honduras, he would have certainly checked in on his old friend. If anyone knew what Simmons was looking for in Central America, it would be Dalton.

Damian stepped onto the dock and made his way to customs while Bertrand unloaded the bags.

To call it a customs office would be culturally sensitive. The hut was at the end of the dock and leaned a little to the left. The ill-fitting door was open to allow the ocean breeze in. Stockwell braced himself as he entered. He held governments in high regard, but he had little use for red tape and it seemed customs houses were held together with it.

Low level officials often possessed a good deal of unnecessary swagger and he wanted to preclude any potential bravado. Damian stood to his full height and entered through the door with authority. "My name is Damian Stockwell and I declare that I am here."

There was no one behind the desk. The customs hut was all but empty.

"And I declare," a voice behind him spoke, "welcome to Honduras."

Stockwell turned and saw his old friend and compatriot Cole Dalton leaning across an open doorway on the opposite end of the shack. Dalton possessed a tall and slender figure that caused his head to brush the doorframe despite the lean. A wide-brimmed straw hat hid his eyes and the majority of his face.

"Dalton, it's been too long."

"Dam, it's good to see you."

Stockwell had no shortage of friends in this world. Among them he counted the members of the lowest castes and the highest ranks of the elite and powerful. He could find a dear friend in any corner of the world. Each was unique. Yet, Cole occupied a special echelon of friendship. Most of his acquaintances were indebted to Damian in some fashion—usually owing their lives to the grand adventurer. With Dalton, the slate was clean. The two men had saved each other's lives so often over the years that they had quit keeping track and merely settled the respective debts with a drink. They had shared adventures around the globe in the pursuit of justice and right and though it had been years since they had seen each other, the small talk was accomplished with a glance, a nod and a punch on the shoulder.

"Ouch. Where are your bags, Dam?"

"Bertrand is fetching them."

"Bertrand? Thought he would have wised up and left you long ago."

"Hardly. Bertrand is as loyal as ever."

"He's a good man. I've got a bunk for both of you at the plantation." Cole stepped toward the door. "We should get going. The bugs get thick at dusk."

Stockwell pointed to the empty desk.

"I've given them the day off. I figured it would be easier for you this way."

"Look at you. Cole Dalton, a man of influence."

Cole chuckled and gestured to the door. "Hardly. I'm just a humble farmer. Now, c'mon. My train is waiting for us."

Damian Stockwell sat in an overstuffed armchair and drew on a cigar so thick that it scared shadows away with every puff. Artwork hung from the walls, the sweet taste of cognac hung in the air and, despite the constant transition the car made from rail to rail, the private train car was relatively quiet. "I'm getting one of these."

"I don't know how I ever lived without one." Cole Dalton dipped the tip of his cigar into his drink and set it back in his mouth.

"Bertrand. Remind me that I must get my own train."

There was no response from the Frenchman but a soft snore.

Dalton chuckled. "Poor fellow seems a bit tuckered."

Stockwell grabbed a rolled up newspaper and rapped the dozing valet on his foot. The snoring continued.

"Bertrand?"

"Oui, Monsieur." Bertrand could not even open his eyes.

"Remind me that I want a train."

"Oui, Monsieur. You want a train."

"Not now, Bertrand. Later, when ..."

The Frenchman's snoring resumed. Stockwell chuckled.

Dalton laughed. "Dam, it's good to see you."

"I know. And look at you. Look at this place. Surrounded by luxury and loyal employees. And, from all appearances, a well-trained security force. You've done good, my friend."

Dalton couldn't help but smile. "Of all our adventures, of all the treasures I've chased, who would have thought I'd find my fortune in fruit?"

"I'm proud of you, Cole."

Bertrand's snore interjected.

"Dammit, Bertrand. Don't interrupt."

"You worked him too hard, Dam. If there's one thing I've learned in this business it's that you can't mistreat your workers."

"Bertrand? The old boy's got it easy. Today was just especially long. I had to kick his ass this morning and then he flew us here. He's earned his rest."

"You beat him?"

"That's actually what brought us here."

Bertrand's snoring grew louder.

"I don't understand."

"I received a distress call yesterday from ..."

Bertrand snorted and the volume of his snoring increased.

"I received a distress call yesterday from ..."

The Frenchman rolled over and the buzzing filled the private car.

"You see, there was this ..."

Bertrand's snoring developed a whistle.

Stockwell leaned forward in his chair and rapped the Frenchman across the shins with the paper. The valet opened his eyes briefly.

"Mind the schnoz, man."

"Je suis désolée." Bertrand turned his back to the men.

"You'll be désolée, all right. I'll make you désolée like you've never been désoléed before. There's a whole level of désolée that you've never even experienced."

The snoring resumed at a lower level. Stockwell raised the paper.

Dalton reached out his hand to stay the strike. "Dam, please continue."

Stockwell leaned back in his chair. "Simmons has disappeared."

"Peter? How do you know this?"

Stockwell pointed to the gold watch on Cole's hand.

Dalton smiled and nodded. "Still, I saw Peter a few days ago. I don't think he's missing. He set off into the jungle with three of my men. He said not to expect him for at least a few weeks."

"So, he was here."

"He was using the plantation as a base camp for an exploration."

Stockwell pulled a pen from his pocket and began to draw on the newspaper.

"I'm sure he's fine, Dam. We both know that Peter can take of himself. Do you remember that time, with the pygmies, when Peter ..."

Stockwell thrust the newspaper in Dalton's face. Dalton jumped at the sight of what Stockwell had drawn. His depiction of the horrid mask was precise. The pain-raked expression, the soulless eyes, every detail had been captured in the field of the crossword puzzle.

"You know this mask." Damian knew from the man's reaction that he had indeed seen the demon face before. Horrid as it was, it would not elicit a start such as Cole's from the image alone.

Dalton nodded.

"This mask arrived in a package for me yesterday. Bertrand placed it on his face and tried to kill me. Several more masked men then attempted to burn, drop, crush and stab me. Simmons now wears this mask."

Stockwell had never known Dalton to hesitate. Countless battles and an equal amount of dangers had never taken the man's words before, but now, Cole paused.

"What is this mask, Cole?"

Dalton's jovial humor faded, he crushed out his cigar and hung his head.

"What is this horrid face?"

"That is the mask of Zipacna."

"That's a stupid name."

"That's his name."

"It's very hard to say."

"But, that's what they call him."

"I'm going to call him Zippy."

"Zipacna ..."

"Zippy."

"... is a Mayan god. That horrid face started appearing a few months ago. At first it was left as mere vandalism on the grounds of the plantation. Then men began to whisper fears in the fields that they were being watched. I dismissed it as native superstition, but, soon after ... they started disappearing. It began with one or two workers a week. Sometimes we would see them return along the perimeter of the plantation wearing the very mask you just showed me. Now, a couple of workers go missing each night. They return aggressive ... almost mindless, and recruit more men. It is a cult, Dam. You measured my wealth in loyal employees, but they have been abandoning me for the promises of some mysterious leader. And I fear what has become of them."

"Are they violent?"

"Only if confronted. Then they attack as if possessed. They hold no reason in their minds. It's as if their very self has been erased and replaced with the spirit of that demon mask."

"Do they attack the plantation? Maybe it was built on sacred ground. Old gods hate that."

"No. The men simply disappear. The ones that remain are terrified. They say that those who do not follow Zipacna's ..."

"Zippy's."

"... call will be drawn in by the crust of the earth itself and brought into his fold. I don't know what to do, Dam."

"Why didn't you call me?"

Dalton smiled and shook his head.

"My friend, there is no shame in asking for help. I know what you're capable of and there's no one I would rather have beside me in a fight. But there are some things that even you or I cannot not handle alone."

"You mean that?"

"I mean, mostly you. I think I'd be all right."

"We tend to handle things ourselves here in Honduras. We'll take care of Zipacna."

Damian smiled. "Zippy. What was Simmons looking for?"

"Gold. The old fool wouldn't listen when I told him there was none. There's nothing in the ground here but bananas. Down here they call them yellow gold."

"But, gold is yellow. So, what do they call gold?"

"Gold."

"Clever."

"Peter insisted there was gold here."

"Are we still talking about bananas?"

"No."

"I follow."

Dalton's head sunk. "I shouldn't have let him go."

Stockwell knew all too well the guilt Dalton was feeling. Even though he himself had written the rule, "The praise and prize of each member's adventure is due to them alone. As is the risk they embrace," into the Vagabond Club charter, he still wrestled with the idea of not helping a friend avoid peril.

"I've failed, Dam. I've failed my friends. I've failed my workers." Dalton drew a heavy breath. "I've failed everyone. They would rather hide behind the face of a long dead god than follow me."

Stockwell stood and put his hand on his old friend's shoulder. "We'll get them back."

"No. They've already decided. There is no turning them back. Each man who wears the mask has become a soulless devil. I've been forced to have my men shoot the cultists on sight. I fear what would happen if their numbers grew. They could threaten the whole of Honduras."

"Cole. There's something you don't know about the masks."

The chatter of submachine fire sounded from above. There was a tremendous bang and the private car was tossed to one side. Stockwell was thrown from his feet. Bertrand fell from his chair. The snoring stopped.

# 17

## All Aboard are Doomed

The private car felt as though it would tip off of the rails. Artwork fell from the walls. The plush chairs slid across the floor tearing the silk carpet as it went. All three men were thrown against the wall. The force of the impact was enough to wake Bertrand and render Cole Dalton unconscious.

Teetering for more than a few seconds, the car balanced at the point of weightlessness. It would take nothing to push it over. There it hung for a perilous moment before finally swaying back into place and dropping heavily on the rails. There was a deafening squeal as the wheels found their place on the tracks.

Bertrand rushed to the window and pulled back the curtain.

Stockwell, pinned by one of the chairs, kicked away the furniture and moved for the door at the rear of the car.

"There are many of them. All on horseback. And, they all have the masks. And they all have ..."

Stockwell opened the door. Before he could step onto the transom, a bladed wooden shaft imbedded itself in the door.

"... spears."

Stockwell ripped the shaft from the door and moved over to Bertrand. "Don't be ignorant, Bertrand. That, my friend, is an atlantl."

Bertrand rolled his eyes. "My apologies."

Gunshots continued to ring out.

Stockwell held up that wooden weapon. "If they're hurling these, it must be Dalton's men that are doing the shooting."

Bertrand peered out the window. "They do not carry guns."

Stockwell dropped the atlantl shaft. "We must stop Dalton's men from killing Dalton's former other men."

"But, they are attacking us."

""These are innocent men, Bertrand. You know better than anyone that the mask has tremendous power over weak minds. These men are not attacking us. It's the doing of their demonic evil overlord—Zippy."

Bertrand shrugged.

"There's no time to waste." With this, Stockwell bent down and snapped the legs from an overturned table. He hoisted the tabletop and moved to the door. With one fluid movement, he opened the door and leapt across the transom to the next car. He landed with his shoulder in the door and knocked it from its hinges. He stood and examined the tabletop. Three atlantl shafts had penetrated deep into the varnished surface.

Stockwell tossed the tabletop back across the void to Bertrand who failed to catch it because of his bandaged hands. The valet shot Damian a cruel look in French.

While Bertrand struggled with picking things up, Stockwell turned his attention to the men in the car. There were two uniformed men. Each was armed with a rifle and both were firing on the train's assailants. They shot with a cadence of trained soldiers.

"Cease fire!"

They did not cease firing.

He grabbed one of the men by the shoulder and pulled him back from the window. "I said stop shooting! The men out there are innocent."

An atlantl shaft tore through the drapes and struck the other man in the shoulder. Blood erupted from the wound as he grabbed at the wooden shaft. He fell away from the window and the rifle clattered to the ground. He screamed in pain, the other soldier pulled away from Stockwell and resumed firing.

Damian pulled the man away from the window. "Son, you need ..." Stockwell drew back as the rifle butt swung near his face. It passed so close under his nose that he could smell the oil on the weapon. The young security guard pointed the rifle at Damian.

"We have orders to shoot these crazies on sight. You have no idea the trouble they've caused."

"But, son, they aren't crazies, they're just not in their right mind. They're innocent men. You need to stop firing now."

"I take my orders from Cole Dalton."

"Cole Dalton is all knocked out."

"Then his standing order stands and we will defend this train at any and all costs."

"Okay then." There was no warning. No signs were telegraphed, but in less than a second Stockwell held the rifle in his hand and the security was knocked out on the floor.

"I'm sorry, son. You've forced my hands."

"Merde, merde, merde, merde." Bertrand came crashing into the car with the tabletop. Several more wooden shafts had stuck into its surface.

Stockwell pulled one out, "Ah, see, Bertrand? This is a spear. You can tell because, unlike the atlantl, there's no place for the sling."

"They are all equally pointy." Bertrand looked to the men on the ground. "What happened here?"

"They wouldn't listen."

"So you stabbed him?" Bertrand bent over to tend to the wounded man.

"No. Well, I guess this one, the knocked out one, didn't listen. This fella just didn't duck."

Stockwell peered out the window. Bertrand had been right. There were nearly three dozen masked men on horseback charging toward the train. Each brandished a primitive weapon. These ranged from the atlantl and spears to daggers and cane knives.

"You're right, Bertrand. There are many. And ... are they naked?"

The men on horseback were bare-chested and bronze from the sun. Their muscles were taut from years of working on the plantation and each was barefoot. Damian watched for a moment and his repulsion faded when he spotted loincloths on the riders.

"Oh, thank goodness for that. I can't stand fighting naked men."

Bertrand placed both of his bandaged hands on the shaft and pulled it out of the man's shoulder. There was a rush of blood, a scream of relief and a weak "thank you" before the man passed out. "He will be okay for now."

Quick clomps of hurried unshod footsteps moved across the roof of the car. The two friends followed the sound from the rear of the car to the front.

Bertrand stood. "This is not a good thing."

Stockwell pointed to the men on the ground. "These men won't listen to reason, Bertrand. They're too loyal to Dalton. And, they're afraid. We're going have to stop this ourselves."

"Oui."

"Now, we have masked men on the roof and security in the cars. I'll take the security team, you take the half-naked natives up there." Stockwell moved to the door. Bertrand stopped him.

"Wait."

"What?"

"Why do you get the men in the cars and I have to face the half-naked ones?"

"You don't like my plan?"

"Non."

"Would you rather flip a coin?"

"Oui. We should flip a coin."

Stockwell reached into his pocket and pulled out a quarter. "Okay. If that's what you want. You flip a coin." He tossed the coin to the valet who tried desperately to catch it.

Light gleamed off the silver coin as it bounced and bobbled between Bertrand's bandaged hands. He stumbled around the car turning, twisting and chasing the airborne currency before he was finally able to catch it between his two gauze-covered palms. The valet laughed and looked to Stockwell.

He was gone. The door to the next car was open and Bertrand could see that Damian had already incapacitated the men. He was heading for the next door, making his way to the engine.

More footsteps sounded above him.

"Merde."

The valet moved to a window opposite the attacking force and kicked out the glass pane. He leaned outside and found rail above him. Though it caused him great pain, he reached up and grabbed the rail. He pulled himself up and rolled onto the roof.

His hands bled through the bandages. It hurt to ball them into fists. It caused such pain that he wondered if all the glass shards had indeed been removed by Damian or his physician. The doctor had warned him that it would not take much to cause nerve damage to such badly cut hands and he should be vigilant to use them as little as possible.

Bertrand stood and looked around the roof. Several masked warriors surrounded him as two more pulled themselves to the top of the train.

The valet sighed and raised his battered hands. He did not ball them up. He could not use them to strike but he would need to for balance.

The first warrior charged. He moved in swiftly waving a vicious looking cane knife. The large flat blade caught all of the sun and caused it to glow.

Bertrand spun and swept wide with his leg and knocked the feet out from under the would-be killer. The masked man landed on his back. Bertrand kicked again and sent the warrior over the edge of the train. He knew that he needed to protect these men's lives, but Stockwell had said nothing of broken limbs.

Before the others could charge, the Frenchman was back on his feet. He stood calmly and tried to peer through the soulless black eyes to see if the attacker really was a man in control of his own faculties. He could see nothing but the lifeless eyes.

Decades of practicing the game from Marseille enabled him to form the perfect savate stance even upon the moving train. As the car swayed back and forth, the Frenchman stood motionless awaiting the perfect moment to strike.

He did not have to wait long.

They all rushed him at once, each wielding a different weapon. Cane knives, rock hammers, machetes—all manner of tools flashed at him as he sprung into action. He was able to use his bandaged hands to deflect blows despite the pain that it caused him, but it was his legs that provided the offensive. Moving in conjunction with his hips, his right leg drove like a piston through the knee of the first masked man.

The attacker dropped instantly. The mask willed him to rise, but a shattered knee was a shattered knee and as the man tried to obey the command of the demon mask, he toppled over the side of the car.

Bertrand landed a second kick square on the chin of another attacker and dislodged the mask. It flew from the worker's face and dissolved into a puff of green mist. Perhaps the man would have realized what had happened and joined the valet in the fight, but the kick struck the nerve cluster on his chin and dropped him to the ground unconscious.

Two more attackers rushed the valet. Quick footwork and a leg sweep sent both over the edge of the car. The final attacker slashed with a machete. Bertrand intercepted the blade with the reinforced sole of his shoe. Damian insisted he wore shoes appropriate for a valet, but Bertrand had seen to it that even his driving boots were prepared for a bout of savate. With the blade deflected, he delivered a final kick straight to the man's jaw.

The masked warrior fell unconscious.

Bertrand could see that the mask had come dislodged, but it still rested on the man's face. Green mist began to escape from the hideous mouth. On the flight, Stockwell had recounted the fight inside the statue and mentioned the disfigurement of the assassin. The Frenchman could not accept such a fate for his attacker. He stepped quickly to the fallen fighter and kicked the mask from his face moments before it dissolved.

The men defeated, Bertrand scanned the area. Behind him, the train was still pursued by men on horseback. Ahead, more masked killers stood on the top of the train cars making their way to the engine. The Frenchman sighed and leapt to the next train car.

Stockwell dashed from car to car, silencing the rifles in each. He gave them each a moment to cease firing, but the men were loyal to their orders and none accepted his offer to "drop it or get kicked in the face." Though he made short work of each man, he felt he would have to compliment Dalton on their training. It was the exception that a security force was so well trained. These men were some of the finest he had encountered. Despite this, they caused him little trouble as he took each down.

As he moved to each car, he heard the scuffle of battle above him on the roof keep pace. Occasionally he saw a body drop to the ground. Damian smiled. Though his hands were useless, his friend was still a fearsome opponent. The Frenchman's footwork above beat a rhythm into the ceiling that could be felt below.

As Stockwell progressed, so did the tune of violence above him. At this rate, the pair should reach the engine at the same time.

Damian crashed through another door. The atlantl and spears had ceased. Stockwell assumed that the raiders had boarded the train or fallen behind. What he assumed was their attempt to derail the train had failed. Their only option was to seize the engine car and try to run it off the tracks.

He increased his pace and cleared two more cars of security guards as they fired into the roof at the footsteps they heard above. Every guard was the same. Local men, they were bronzed skin, dark haired and possessed brown eyes that grew wide as Stockwell apologized for beating them into submission. It all began to feel redundant until he reached the final car.

The guard was the size of a gorilla and stood almost to the height of the ceiling. He fired a .45 automatic into the roof.

"Cease fire. That's my friend up there."

"The Cult of Zipacna is on my train."

"Bertrand will take care of them. He's very ... kicky."

"Kicking is too good for these traitors."

"Stop now or I'll be forced to stop you."

"Try it, little man." The guard pulled another clip from his belt and moved to reload the .45.

Stockwell grabbed a plate setting from a nearby table and hurled it across the car. It landed true in between the gun and clip.

The guard grunted in frustration as he dropped the plate.

Damian crashed into the mountainous man with all of his fury and the guard toppled to the ground.

The large Honduran shoved Stockwell off of him with such force that the intrepid adventurer landed on his feet. The guard grabbed Damian's ankle and pulled his feet from under him.

Stockwell rolled back into a defensive stance as the guard attacked.

It had been his experience that large men such as this did not strike with fists, they rarely kicked, they merely sought to grab and squeeze the life from their opponents. This man was no different.

Large hands grasped for his neck. Stockwell dropped beneath the grapple and struck the man above the groin and triggered a reflex in his diaphragm.

Air rushed from the large man's lungs as he doubled over. Stockwell rolled onto his back and drove both feet into the man's chin. The guard stumbled backwards on the brink of unconsciousness but did not succumb. His hands flailed for support as he fought for balance and found the edge of a table. A fierce tear later and the tabletop was in his hands. With a tremendous growl, the guard drove his own head through the solid wood and snapped it in two. He came at Stockwell with a splintered plank in each hand.

The air around the boards shrieked as it was torn by the flying wood. Damian was forced back as he ducked and dodged the makeshift cudgels. They drew closer with each pass and he was running out of room. As he scrambled, he felt blindly for anything that he could use as a weapon. There was nothing.

He rolled back as one of the boards came crashing down. His only hope was to get to the doorway. The frame would limit the strikes the guard could employ and give him a fighting chance.

Damian sprung to his feet and opened the door. There stood the somewhat groggy but awake Cole Dalton.

"Humberto, stop."

The massive mauler ceased his attack at the order of his employer. He dropped the boards but did not move.

"Let him pass."

Humberto grunted and stepped aside. Damian could explain the effects of the masks later. Dalton undoubtedly trusted his actions. Stockwell dashed past the guard. He had to protect the engine from the invaders.

He rushed into the tank engine. The engineer fired. A bullet ricocheted close to Damian's head. He dropped into a crouch with his palms out.

"Lo siento." The engineer lowered the gun.

Damian could tell the man was frightened. He nodded to accept the apology and spoke to him in his native Spanish. "It's okay, my friend. I'm here to help."

A look of relief crossed the man's face for but a moment.

A hiss passed overhead and the engineer grabbed for his throat. He pulled a small barb from his neck, looked at it for a moment and fell to the ground.

Stockwell looked up through the open roof and saw the attacker. His mask was different than the others. In place of the hideous grimace, the lips of the mask were puckered as if to draw water from a stream. The figure above placed something in the lips and removed his hands.

Damian moved behind the bulkhead as another barb spit from the mask. It bounced harmlessly off the steel. He rolled for the engineer's gun. As he drew to fire, a well-tailored boot wrapped around the mask's face and struck the spitter into the engine bay.

Dalton and Humberto rushed through the doorway.

"Hold him, but do not remove his mask," Stockwell yelled as he checked the pulse of the engineer.

Humberto grabbed the man by the throat and held him over the passing landscape. The masked man struggled against the firm grip.

"No! I need to examine that mask."

Humberto could not hear or did not care. The man's legs kicked as he struggled at the grip of the massive guard. Humberto was smiling.

"Dalton! Tell him to listen."

Cole would trust him. The two had been through too much together.

Dalton nodded, "Humberto, set him down."

The large Honduran was not happy but nodded his compliance.

There was a shrill whistle and Humberto screamed as a barb imbedded itself beneath his eye. He lost his grip and the masked man fell free from the train and to the ground below. Humberto pulled the barb from his eye. The massive Honduran stumbled. He reached out for support but could find none. He collapsed to the floor.

"Dam, what is going on here?"

"He'll be okay. The darts are not fatal."

"Why did you beat up all of my men?"

"Your workers are not traitors, Dalton. They are victims of ..."

"Zipacna."

"Zippy, right."

"No." Cole Dalton pushed passed Stockwell and pointed through the thick glass of the engine. There, ahead on the tracks, stood a massive figure draped in flowing robes and wearing a mask twice the size of the attackers. The figure did not move, but stood firm in front of the oncoming train. "Zipacna."

Stockwell's eyes narrowed and he breathed the maniac's name. "Zippy?"

Dalton pushed Stockwell aside and grabbed the train's throttle. He pushed it to its forward and the engine let out a blast of steam.

"What are you doing?" Stockwell grabbed for the lever.

"He must die."

"No. We need him alive if we're to save these men." Damian reached for the brake.

Dalton pushed him back.

Damian reached in again.

His friend pulled a gun. "I'm sorry, Dam. He must be stopped."

Together the two men had faced down the grim killer that was the Madman of Macau. As a team they had stopped the

horrific Cannibals of Calcutta. And only their combined bravery
had been enough to put a stop to the mystic killings of the
Abomination of Albania. Never had he seen terror in his friend's
eyes. But, there it was. It was fear that had pulled the weapon, not
his friend. It was fright that forced Dalton to open the train's
throttles.

"Dalton, don't."

"Stay back, Dam!"

Bertrand dropped from the roof of the car onto the gun in
Dalton's hand and knocked the man to the ground. The weapon
discharged and shattered the engine's windscreen. The Frenchman
pinned Cole to the ground and Stockwell leapt for the brakes.

He pulled the lever back and let up on the throttle, but it was
too late. The powerful steam engine was moving too fast.

Bertrand stood and looked through the window at the
imposing figure of Zipacna. Dalton stood and screamed at the
Mayan god as his locomotive barreled down upon him.

Stockwell watched in amazement. The engine was upon him
and still the villainous Zippy made no move to clear the tracks.
"He's mad!"

Soon there was no time. Even if he had been the one
standing in its path, Stockwell could not react fast enough to dodge
the train. Zipacna was going to be run down and no force on Earth
could stop it.

Then, the moment before impact, the large robed figure
erupted in a cloud of green mist. His form disappeared in the cloud
of emerald haze. The mist splashed against the front of the train
and dispersed into the Honduran countryside.

The three men stared in silence, each not wanting to admit
what they had seen. For a moment there was only the chug of the
engine until Bertrand spoke.

"Mon dieu. That was creepy."

# 18

## A Worn Out Summer's Evening

Whether he was ashamed of his actions or "sleepy" as he claimed, Dalton retired to his quarters immediately upon their arrival at the plantation. Stockwell wished to speak with his friend further but had learned when to give the man his space.

The fear he had seen in Dalton's eyes worried him. Together they had faced horrors unknown until the point they were known. In their experience together they had discovered that no matter how supernatural occurrences seemed, in the end the events exposed a rational explanation. Whether Dalton had forgotten this or if he had let his perceived failure cloud his judgment was not clear. Few men were as loyal as Cole Dalton and seeing his workers succumb to the "supernatural" could have had devastating effects on his psyche.

Stockwell swatted at a mosquito that had made the poor decision to land on his neck. This is when it occurred to him that the environment could have played a part in Dalton's collapse. It was miserable in the jungle and he had been here for far too long. He had worked hard to build his business and probably needed a vacation.

Once this mystery was solved and Simmons was rescued, he would see to it that Dalton returned to the States for a well-deserved and much less humid rest.

Humberto had recovered from the poisoned barb. As Stockwell had suspected, the poison was not lethal but merely induced a temporary paralysis in its victim. The engineer, a much smaller man than the monstrous security guard, was awake but still groggy from its effects. The large Honduran had simply recovered angrier than before and had been tasked with showing Stockwell and Bertrand to their quarters.

The main plantation home looked as if it belonged in the American South more so than Central America. White columns supported the roof over a large porch that surrounded the palatial home. The large estate held both the working offices of the All-American Banana Company and the executive's residence.

Dalton's quarters occupied the entire third floor of the mansion. Damian and Bertrand were shown to separate rooms on the west wing of the second floor.

Stockwell's mind was flush with questions from the day's events and he needed someone with which to volley theories. After seeing to his luggage, he crossed the hall to Bertrand's quarters. The Frenchman had passed out on the bed, having barely crawled inside the mosquito netting. He still wore his clothes.

"That's just sloppy, Bertrand."

Still, his loyal companion could have been on to something. Rest was a weapon in the fight against both evil and weariness. Though he had slept on the Dahlia, fighting a well-trained security force had worn him out as well. Now, having seen the full force of the enemy, he knew he would need every advantage to emerge victorious in this particular skirmish against the forces of evil.

"Sleep well, my friend. You've earned your rest for the day."

The Frenchman did not stir.

Stockwell looked at his friend. Blood soaked his bandaged hands and threatened to stain the white linen sheets. Damian sighed and moved to the luggage. Bertrand always carried a doctor's satchel wherever they traveled. Stockwell found it and removed several rolls of fresh gauze and a bottle of iodine.

"What would you do without me to take care of you, Bertrand?"

Damian pulled back the mosquito netting and rolled his friend over to tend to his wounds. Bertrand's eyes were still open.

"Bertrand?" At first Stockwell thought the valet was playing him. He half expected a smile to emerge. But there was no alertness in the valet's eyes. Stockwell snapped his fingers several times and received no response. He slapped the man several times across the cheek. Still only a vacant stare gazed back at him. That's when he saw the tiny barb sticking from the Frenchman's neck. He pulled it free and examined it. Bertrand had not passed out like some goldbrick, he had been drugged.

Damian trained his senses as much as his impressive muscles and now they served him well. In the dark beyond the open window was a masked figure with terribly pouty lips. The dark wood of the mask blended into the shadows and did not move. Had it been anyone else, the figure would have gone unnoticed.

"You coward!" Stockwell's booming voice did not shake the man in the window. Instead, the hideous face leaned in closer and blew. There was a pffft and a thwip.

Stockwell intercepted the barb with Bertrand's hand.

The mask blew several more times unleashing a slew of poisoned needles into the air from the blowgun integrated in its face.

Stockwell was a blur of motion as he swung Bertrand's hands. He intercepted each dart and dropped the valet's limp limbs.

The mask was out of ammo and the figure faded into the darkness of the night.

"Not so fast, perpetrator!" Damian leapt across the bed and scrambled for the window. He became momentarily entangled in the mosquito netting and hopped a few steps to shake it free from his leg.

The sheer fabric would not release its hold.

Stockwell so loved justice that even this mere hindrance drove him into a rage. He kicked his leg violently left and right in the hopes to shake free from the net's hold, but its grip was too entwined.

Damian screamed and gave a mighty tug. The fabric ripped at the bed post and the grand adventurer was free again. He rushed to the window and peered into the darkness.

There was no moon this night and the multitude of stars did little to light the ground below him. Still, he leapt. He soared from the second story window with the netting trailing behind him. Landing with a roll, he absorbed the force of the fall and converted it to forward momentum. His feet beat craters into the fertile soil as he dashed across the manicured grounds of the plantation home. His eyes were open for the slightest movement. His ears were attuned to the faintest sound. There was a large crash directly ahead of him as the masked man charged into the jungle.

Stockwell crashed after him. The jungle canopy blocked out even the faint starlight and he was forced to rely on his hearing to continue the pursuit. Bare feet against harsh ground made a distinctive sound. He focused only on this and blocked out the sounds of the insects, the movement of the animals in the treetops and a ripping sound that he couldn't quite identify.

The footsteps were getting fainter. The blow-gunman was increasing his lead. The mask's effect on the man's nervous system had once again put Stockwell at a disadvantage. For a moment the sounds of feet against bare earth and foliage turned to that of someone running on gravel. Then they disappeared. Stockwell charged on, instinctively swatting branches and vines from his path until he could no longer hear anything.

He stopped and stared into the darkness while straining to hear any sound made by man. There was a distant crash and Stockwell dashed towards it. To his surprise, he emerged in a clearing. Before it could register, he had also tripped on a railroad tie.

The massive man of good fell to the ground on a set of railroad tracks. His befuddlement lasted only a moment as he realized how close he had come to becoming his own downfall. He had caught his fall with his right arm and almost landed on his fist. The same right fist that held the poisoned barb. It had been a mere inch from puncturing his chest.

He rose to his feet and stood silent and still. There was no sound around him. He had lost the masked man. It enraged him that he had no one to blame but himself, but Bertrand was still unconscious on the bed. Once resigned to this fact, he examined the rail line. They had not been in place long, the rails still shone free of rust. They were too narrow a gauge for a passenger or freight train. This track had been laid for a special purpose. He intended to discover it. Tracks always led somewhere and he hoped that these would lead him to another clue in Simmons's disappearance and the origin of the horrid masks.

# 19

## Train Tracks Bound for Nowhere

The tracks were level and the ground beneath them packed well. This was no amateur setup. Stockwell moved down the line stepping from trestle to trestle, always aware of the sounds around him. At any moment the masked man could reemerge with a new face full of poisoned darts.

His gait and demeanor, however, were purposefully set to draw the man out of hiding. To the casual observer, Stockwell appeared to be a pre-teen strolling the tracks for lack of something better to do. Occasionally, he walked the rail itself foot-before-foot acting as if his balance was in jeopardy.

After twenty minutes, the bait was taken. Stockwell was skipping a trestle with each step when he heard the noise behind him. The footfall itself made no sound. It was a slight shift in the gravel that caught his attention. Stockwell pivoted and sprung his own trap.

"Aha."

There was a deafening roar.

"OhGodbigcat!"

The jaguar, black from head to toe, leapt. The slight moonlight shimmered off the pitch black fur like strands of silk drifting through the air. Its claws were extended; its teeth bared.

The two-hundred-pound beast crashed into him and the two collapsed to the ground with Stockwell underneath. He looked into the jaws of the creature as it roared its intent. The beast's face was so close to his own that he could smell the rotting flesh of an earlier kill.

Damian grabbed the predator by the neck and rolled. The pair moved across the tracks and broke apart. The distance was not enough. The jaguar's ability to leap outshone his own. There was no tree Stockwell could climb that would provide a sanctuary from the fierce predator. The trees were its hunting ground as much as the jungle floor.

The two circled each other, staring into one another's eyes seeking an opening. Damian could see the arrogance in the cat's eyes. It had always sat atop the food chain and feared nothing. As Stockwell studied the cat's movements trying to anticipate the attack, the beast merely looked at him as dinner.

Damian crouched low. Conventional wisdom said that one should try to look as large as possible to frighten the creature into a retreat. But, this creature did not know fear. There was nothing in the jungle that could be considered a threat to this savage apex predator. There would be no scaring this beast.

Stockwell was ready to protect his head. The jaguar had a disturbingly unique attack amongst big cats—it would often forgo the victim's neck, skipping the jugular and opting instead to pierce its victim's skull with its large, sharp fangs.

The cat roared, possibly hoping for a reaction from its prey. Stockwell kept his stance. He did not flinch.

The cat sprung. Coiled muscles launched the six-foot beast through the humid night air and the cat landed upon Damian, dragging them both to the gravel bed of the tracks.

The jaguar went for its killing strike and bit for Stockwell's head.

Damian brought up his hand and shoved it deep into the hunter's mouth.

The cat let out a startled chirp and backed away from its prey.

Its face stretched. Its mouth opened and shut rapidly as if it was trying to speak. It coughed several times, let out a yelp and fell over onto the railroad track.

Stockwell rose to his feet and approached the fallen beast. He reached down and scratched behind its ears. "Good kitty." Damian crouched and reached back into the cat's mouth. He pulled out the barb and tossed it into the jungle. He hefted the cat onto his shoulder and stepped off the tracks.

A rare black jaguar pelt would be quite the trophy for most men, but Stockwell respected everything in this world that tried to kill him. He couldn't leave the cat on the tracks for fear it did not wake before the next car passed. He found a tree nearby and set the jaguar in the crotch of two branches. The big cat would rest peacefully and awaken confused, possibly hungry, but unharmed.

The cat's presence had done two things. One, it had startled him, and two, it had confirmed that the masked warrior was not close. Had two men been in the area, the cat would have remained hidden.

Stockwell quickened his pace. There was no telling how deep the rail line went into the jungle. The sooner he found the source, the sooner he could get out from among the bugs.

He jogged at a brisk pace for more than an hour before he wondered if he had chosen the wrong direction. He stopped for a moment and sat on the rail, the cool steel was a welcomed sensation and he lay down to place his face against it. He hated the sweltering heat of the jungle.

A moment later he placed his hand on the rail. It was faint, but there was a vibration on the track. He placed his ear to the tie. There was definitely something approaching. Whatever was causing it was either very distant or much smaller than a train. A moment later Damian had his answer.

The exhaust of a v-twin engine drifted around a bend in the track. Damian stepped off of the rail line and ducked into the jungle. The bugs instantly set upon him. He slapped at each carefully enough to kill the offending insect but not make contact with his skin and give away his position.

For the first time since setting out, the jungle around him was illuminated. A small headlamp on the vehicle made shadows dance but could not penetrate deep into the foliage. The vehicle was a motorcycle that had been converted to ride on the tracks. Stripped of its tires, the rims connected directly to the rail. Jutting from the side of the bike, an arm extended to the far rail to provide balance.

It moved quickly around the corner. The rider was hunched over the handlebars to increase his speed. As he passed, Stockwell could see the mask on his face. The bike moved out of sight and was soon out of earshot as well. Damian stepped back onto the track.

"Brilliant. That explains how they get around so fast."

Stockwell resumed his jog. The track went unchanged for another mile. There he found a spur line that ran off into the darkness. He could only guess where it led.

He increased his pace. How long had he been following the tracks now? The sun was beginning to make its presence known. The blackness of the jungle changed into several shades of blackness. He was miles from the plantation and with no end in sight.

Around the next bend, the end came into sight. Stockwell stopped and muttered, "Well, that's not what I expected at all."

The sun rose behind an ancient Mayan temple. Little of the structure was visible as nature had seen fit to reclaim the pyramid with thick vines and invasive roots. The outline of the pyramid could barely be distinguished from the rainforest beyond. Stockwell had visited many pre-Columbian sites and his trained eye estimated the size of the construction. He had never seen a temple on this scale. The interior chambers could hold untold treasures had it remained undisturbed, but an opening at its base proved that he was not the first to discover the site. The vines had been cleared and the rail line ran inside.

Stockwell stepped off the tracks and approached the entrance with caution. There were no guards visible but the jungle hid many secrets. He found cover and observed the temple for several minutes before moving in.

The interior of the temple was a mix of the old world and the new. The chamber was lit with incandescent bulbs powered by a generator that hummed in the center of the room. Intricate carvings lined the stone walls and depicted stories that had been lost to antiquity. Though he was unfamiliar with Mayan symbols, Stockwell quickly recognized the temple's central theme.

"So this is your place, Zippy."

At the center of each carving was one figure—Zipacna. Each wall told a tale. The rear wall depicted two groups of people. On the right, the masses offered tribute. On the left they placed nothing before the god. The wall to the right showed the bounty for the faithful as Zipacna opened the earth and poured riches upon them. The wall to the left showed the penalty for insolence. The ground had opened up beneath them and people screamed as they were swallowed by the earth.

"You're quite the pill, Zippy."

The ancient carvings stood in stark contrast to the rest of the chamber's contents. Several more of the converted cycles were lined up against the wall. Power cables ran across the floor and down a hallway. Lights were placed every twenty feet, and, still, Damian could not see the end of the hallway from the chamber—it ran too far and too deep.

Stockwell turned to the carving of Zipacna. "Mind if I show myself around?"

He crept down the hallway. The grade was steep and declined two to three feet for every ten in length. The floor was ancient stone and he walked softly to keep his footsteps silent. The noise would carry forever inside the temple and he was not yet ready to make his presence known.

After a hundred feet, the path turned right. Stockwell continued on for another seventy-five yards before the tunnel wound left. Fifty feet later, the stone floor turned to earth. The stone walls turned to shoring timbers. The tunnel wound twice more. A sudden hiss stopped him. It came from the tunnel ahead. It sounded like a burst of steam. A crash followed. A few moments later he heard the sound of toil.

He reached the end of the tunnel and it all became clear. The temple was an adit. Zipacna was the Mayan earth god and his temple led to this—the tunnel opened up to a massive cavern filled with masked workers digging for gold.

No less than five dozen stood in a pit. Without a sound they bent over and picked up nuggets from a pile on the ground. They placed the precious metal on a conveyor belt which ran further into the cavern. As Stockwell watched, he wondered how the gold was torn from the earth. None of the men held picks. There were no drills or jackhammers evident. The mine was eerily silent.

The men finished scrounging the floor of the cavern and all but one climbed from the pit. The remaining worker approached the wall holding what looked like a flamethrower, but the tanks on his back were larger than any model Stockwell had seen. They were massive and he doubted that any man could hoist them if not under the influence of the mask.

The worker aimed at the cavern wall and released a stream of green fluid. Damian recognized it as the same substance discharged from the assassin's weapon. The stream spread across the wall and instantly began to hiss. Before his eyes, the acid ate away the rock and earth.

The worker ceased firing. The wall continued to hiss and decay. The liquid turned to a green mist and drafted towards the roof of the cavern. Where rock had been, gold dust fluttered to the ground like snowflakes. Larger nuggets dropped from the wall and the workers moved back into the pit to collect the gold.

This impossible chemical was a breakthrough in science. Stockwell mused that it would be worth more on the market than the gold that was being pulled from the mine. Whoever was behind this insidious plot had obviously lost all sense. Throughout history gold fever had driven many mad and the brilliant mastermind of the horrific masks was no different.

The mining was not concentrated in a single pit. The operation was enormous. Wooden gangplanks and scaffolding littered the massive cavern. Teams of masked men worked together to spray the acid and collect the gold. Others still were set to various tasks.

Some pushed ore carts. Others constructed more scaffolding from rope and timber. In the center of it all a group of men mixed chemicals into a large vat that boiled with an eerie green glow. Each man was focused solely on his job—the masks demanded it. This focus served Damian and enabled him to move about the cavern without much scrutiny.

He kept to the shadows of the walls and explored the workings of the cavern.

He passed a series of men sorting through the rubble on the conveyor belt. They tossed out any rock that had not been dissolved by the acid wash and left only gold running down the belts to awaiting ore carts. Another group constructed more masks that would in turn possess new victims and turn them to slaves. He moved closer to the assembly area and observed.

As he suspected, the masks were not solid. Each was hollow, the face merely a veneer of an element he could not place. When the pieces were assembled, the workers attached a small hose fed by another tank of acid. When the worker released the hose, there was a small pfft that told Damian the contents were pressurized.

Once filled, the mask was turned over. A separate worker approached with a mass of wires soldered to a small board. It was set into the back of the mask and bolted in.

The magic had been revealed. It was science after all. Once several masks were assembled, another slave loaded them in a tray and left the area.

Stockwell followed this man to a darkened corner of the cave. The masked laborer disappeared into a redoubt. For the first time since entering the temple, Stockwell heard a human's voice. It was weak and raspy. It was barely human at all.

"You coward. You can't ..."

There was silence. A minute passed before he heard the voice again.

"You can fight this. You can ...."

Silence once more.

Stockwell entered the tunnel. Back in the shadows he could see a masked man tied to the cave wall. He hung limp at first but suddenly sprang to life when the mask was removed. He began to plea.

"Please. Fight the ..."

The worker placed another mask on the prisoner.

The shackled man fell silent once more. The worker removed the mask and reached for another. He was testing the effectiveness of each.

The prisoner became conscious once more. This time he lunged forward to the length of his shackles and growled at the man.

Stockwell charged in. The man on the wall was his friend, Peter Simmons.

# 20

## Met Up with a Mayan

Quality assurance was the worker's only task and, aside from falling to the ground unconscious, he did not react when Damian kicked him in the head.

Stockwell grabbed one of the new masks and pulled a knife from his pocket. He flipped open the blade and punched a hole in the mask's veneer. The gas sprayed instantly and he pointed the puncture at the chains that held his friend to the wall.

The thick-gauged links snapped without a sound and Simmons fell to the floor of the cave. Stockwell grabbed his friend and helped him to his feet. Simmons rose but was otherwise unresponsive.

"Simmons?" Stockwell slapped his friend's face.

"Get away. Get away. Fight it. Fight it." Simmons babbled to himself and slumped to the ground.

"Simmons, it's me. Dam." He tapped the man's cheek. "Simmons?" Repeated exposure to the mask's hypnotic effect had taken its toll on the man. Simmons was awake but hardly alert. His eyes were open but they did not focus. "Let's get you out of here, old friend."

Damian lifted Simmons from the ground and draped the man's arm over his neck. He checked the man's feet. Simmons supported his own weight but was still unaware of his surroundings.

"Fight it. Fight it!" Simmons began to scream. His madness would make sneaking out more difficult than it had been sneaking in. Stockwell looked up and saw what Simmons was shouting at.

The entrance to the tunnel was choked with masked workers. They were no longer occupied by their errands. Each looked at him with soulless black eyes but did not move. Their sheer numbers made moving from the tunnel impossible. Stockwell was trapped.

"You men can fight this. It's not you. I know it's not you. The mask you wear has not robbed you of free will, only buried it deep in lies and science. If each of you look deep inside, you can find that spark that will overtake its power. You can be free men."

There was no response. They only stared and stood as human roadblocks between Stockwell and freedom.

"I'm warning you men to move."

Without a sound, the center of the tunnel emptied. Workers filed with drill like precision to the side of the cavern walls and formed a pathway of creepy stares. Stockwell was used to being obeyed but even he had to admit that he was surprised that the men listened. He shrugged his shoulders, assumed it was his commanding presence that had moved the men and helped Simmons down the pathway.

"No!" Simmons cried out, his knees buckled and he fell to the ground.

"Simmons, this really isn't helpful. I know I didn't tell you but I ran a long way to get here. I fought a cat. I could really use some help."

Simmons scrambled back on all fours into the cave.

Stockwell turned and found himself staring into a cloaked chest. He looked up at the hideous face; it was the same as on the temple walls.

Stockwell nodded. "Zippy."

The large figured loomed over the mighty adventurer. For a long moment he was silent. Then a raspy voice, low and powerful, emanated from the mask.

"These men are not free. They obey my will, not yours."

"And who are you to enslave these men?"

"I am Zipacna, lord of the Earth's crusts. I have dominion over the crops, the wells and the riches you see here. And I will soon have dominion over you, the mighty Damian Stockwell."

Damian smiled, "Oh, you've heard of me. I must say I'm a little shocked since I don't hang out in the Earth's crust much these days. I'm really more of a surface man myself."

"Silence, mortal."

Mortal? "Hey."

Zipacna turned and walked slowly out of the tunnel. "Bring them."

The workers flooded in and the tunnel closed once more. Stockwell raised his fists and grit his teeth. He charged into the throng of bodies.

They closed in on him. He landed only one strike before he found his arms pinned. No one had restrained him, but the crowd was so thick that he could not move. He struggled to free himself but the mass of people had swallowed him. His arms were pinned to his side. His feet were lifted from the ground. Even his chest was constricted and he found himself struggling to breathe.

Each worker stunk of months in the mines. Perspiration dripped from their bodies and mixed with the filth that had accumulated from their labors. Stockwell was repulsed by it all. He hadn't had this much gritty, sweaty flesh pressed against him since he had faced the Sadistic Sumo of the Sudan.

The crowd moved and carried him with them. He quickly realized it would be a waste of energy to struggle against the mob. He would need to bide his time. Damian stopped struggling and began biding.

Behind him, Simmons struggled and screamed. What horrors this man must have been exposed to in his time in the cave. To have one's mind taken repeatedly from one's own control was sure to drive one mad. Then, to throw him into a group of sweaty half-naked men ... the mind could only take so much.

Like the digestive tract of a snake, they passed the pair to the front of the mob. Stockwell and Simmons were dropped next to each other at the feet of Zipacna. Stockwell stood. Simmons collapsed.

"Your friend knows his place. Kneel before me."

"I don't do the whole kneeling thing."

Zipacna wheezed. The sound was weak behind the mask but it sounded like a panting. Stockwell soon realized it to be laughter.

"I think the air in here might be getting to you, Zippy. You may need to see a good ear, nose and throat guy."

The Mayan god stepped closer. Stockwell's impressive stature did not even rise to shoulder height on the massive figure. Zipacna continued to laugh. "I've always enjoyed this American arrogance."

It was Stockwell's turn to chuckle. "Watch what you say about America, pal. This arrogance is pure Stockwell."

"Ah, yes. The mighty Stockwell. Even your mind will break. Look around you. All of these men believed they possessed free will. Each thought they alone could control their actions. But they, like you, are feeble-minded simpletons. Free will is nothing compared to the power of a god."

"God, schmod. I saw your science. You're no deity. You're just a man in a mask, like everyone else here."

Zipacna leaned in closer. For the first time Stockwell could see the details of the hideous mask. He looked close at the glassy eyes and the gnarled teeth. It sat upon a flowing cape that closed tight around Zipacna's chest. A large gold hasp kept the cloak around his impossibly wide shoulders.

"I am their god. Their minds belong to me. I control these men and soon there will be many more. By now, all of the workers at the plantation are under my control."

"You fiend. Only a coward would feed his need for power by stealing freedom."

"Freedom is a weak ideal."

"Freedom is the most powerful force on earth."

"In a moment you'll no longer believe that. You won't believe anything. I will do your thinking for you."

"Not me, Zippy." Stockwell tapped his head. "Nobody gets up here but me."

"Yes, the mighty mind of Stockwell. They say it's unbreakable. Well, I have carved a special mask just for you." Zipacna reached into his cloak and pulled out a mask. It was different than the rest. It was silly looking. The fierce look was replaced with bulging eyes that pointed in two different directions. The cheeks were plump. The chin wasn't cleft and the tongue hung down one side of a goofy grin.

"I'd look like a fool in that thing."

"Precisely."

Zipacna leaned in and turned the mask towards Damian.

There was a scream and Zipacna's attention was drawn to the cavern entrance.

A masked worker tumbled from the tunnel and into the mine.

Stockwell smiled. "Way to go, Bertrand."

Bertrand ran into the cavern and charged towards the crowd.

Zipacna waved his hand, "Stop him."

Half of the mob responded without a sound and rushed to end the Frenchman's assault. The other half closed in around Stockwell and Simmons to prevent an escape.

Bertrand's feet caused the wooden walkways to shake as he ran from platform to platform. The first worker to reach him received a boot to the face. The second, a knee. The Frenchman's feet were deadly but they did little to deter the brainwashed mass of workers that was soon upon him.

Bertrand tried to climb a scaffold to escape the mob but could not get a grip without his hands. Several surrounded him at the base of the structure. They came at him.

French feet and knees flew as the valet ducked in and out of the timber scaffold. Between each strike he pulled his hands to his mouth. Gnashing with his teeth, he tore the end of each bandage free.

With every spin kick and forearm block, the bandages unraveled. As he delivered the brutal strikes, his hands became free. The bloody gauze twirled around him as he spun and countered attacks. Before long they spiraled around him like the ribbon of a gymnast's floor exercise, but much less lame. He used these, too, as a weapon to distract and confuse the miners and his would be killers.

Once able to ball his fists, he became unstoppable. Foot and fist combinations shattered masks, upended workers and brought pain to the face of men that had felt nothing for months. He leapt into the scaffolding and used the complex supports to dodge and destroy his attackers.

Stockwell struggled to join him, but the sweaty mob held the mighty adventurer in place. All he could do was watch Bertrand as the Frenchman climbed to the top of the scaffold.

The mob followed. Masked killers climbed the structure while others at the base began to shake the structure.

Bertrand gave Stockwell a quick glance and drew Damian's gun from the sheath on his back.

"Well, Zippy," Stockwell said calmly.

Zipacna turned to Stockwell.

Stockwell smiled. "This is where we say good-bye."

Bertrand pulled the trigger. The massive .357 barked louder than ever before. The report bounced off the cavern walls and found only other walls. The mining process had created multiple echo chambers and the gunshot found each one of them before bouncing back to the center again. The rock surface multiplied the blast into a deafening roar.

The intensity of the sound was unreal. The masked men reached for their ears and fell to the ground.

Stockwell lunged forward and punched Zipacna in the chest directly below the golden hasp. His fist connected with a man's jaw beneath the robes. Zipacna collapsed to the ground.

"Ha. I knew your face was there. I knew it."

The report faded and the workers began to rise. They placed themselves between Stockwell and their deity. Zipacna fled.

Bertrand fired a second shot into the air and the mob dropped again.

"Let's go, Simmons." Stockwell helped his friend to his feet and the two rushed through the fallen crowd, not necessarily trying their best to avoid stepping on hands or kicking random miners.

It wasn't long before the workers tried to stand and Bertrand was forced to fire again.

The Frenchman made his way down the scaffold and met the pair at its base. He had been forced to fire three more shots to cover their escape.

"It's good to see you, Bertrand. But how did you find me?"

From his pocket, Bertrand produced a torn piece of sheer white fabric. "I don't know what that is. Is it a French thing?"

"It is mosquito netting."

Stockwell smiled. "Nice work, my friend. Now we've got to get back to the plantation. If Zippy was telling the truth, we have to save a lot of people."

Bertrand unslung the sheath from his back and handed the weapon to Stockwell. "You should tell your friend it's too loud."

Stockwell smirked and took the weapon. The two friends ran up the tunnel with Simmons between them. They moved into the chamber as the mob behind them began to rise.

# 21

## Know When to Run

Stockwell burst into the temple alcove and tackled the masked guard to the ground before the sentry could turn around. The guard's face struck the carvings on the wall and the mask cracked in two. Damian pulled the worker back from the mist before it could corrode his face.

Another guard stepped behind the mighty adventurer and locked a wiry arm under the blond titan's neck.

Damian grabbed the wrist and tried to pull it free, but the science of the mask, and years climbing banana trees, had given the man tremendous strength. Stockwell stepped back and rolled the worker over his shoulder using one of the many Judo moves he had incorporated into Damitsu. The worker fell to the ground. Stockwell kicked him in the head until he was unconscious, using one of the dirtier moves he had incorporated into Damitsu.

Bertrand emerged from the tunnel with Simmons hanging from one shoulder. Stockwell rushed by them, searching for a way to seal the tunnel entrance. He could hear the mob of masked madmen moving up the grade toward them. There was nothing: no lever to pull, no pile of rubble to collapse, no door to close. There was only a wide open space and hundreds of brainwashed warriors scientifically infused with bloodlust. "He keeps a clean cave, that Zippy."

"Monsieur, what should I do with him?" Blood ran down Bertrand's hands and forearms. Every stitch must have broken during the melee in the cavern and the trailing bandages were doing nothing to ebb the flow of blood or protect the wounds from infection.

Stockwell glanced around the antechamber. Modified motorcycles and ore carts lined the walls. Each bike was like the one that had passed him in the night—stripped of its tires and custom fitted with a support bar for the second rail. In the light of the day, he could also see a hitch on the back of each bike. Damian grabbed an ore cart and rolled it towards Bertrand, "Put him in there."

The valet dropped Simmons in the cart and rushed to the tunnel entrance. The Frenchman began to bounce back and forth on the balls of his feet—readying himself for the fight ahead. "They are coming, Monsieur."

Stockwell lifted a motorcycle and placed it on the rail in front of the cart. Simmons was conscious but hardly alert. He muttered pleas as if he were still shackled to the wall. Stockwell kicked a latch on the cart. It fell into place and attached the ore cart to the cycle at the hitch. He kick-started the engine. "On the bike, Bertrand."

The valet leapt onto the bike and engaged the clutch.

"Just keep the throttle open and the bike on the rails. You've got to get Simmons to safety."

"Where are you going?"

"I've got to get back to the plantation. Zippy sent a bunch of his men to capture everyone there. If he masks those soldiers, he'll have an army of trained killers under his command."

"How will I get ..."

"Trust me, old friend. Just go. I'm right behind you."

Bertrand released the clutch and the motorcycle's rim spun on the rail. Sparks flew before the rim took hold and launched the bike down the track with the ore cart and Simmons in tow.

Damian could hear the mob nearing the antechamber. They would be on him in seconds. He dashed to the line of motorcycles, leapt into the air and brought his boot down on the muffler. The light metal buckled and he kicked at it several more times to shear the equipment from the exhaust line.

The mob burst into the antechamber. Arms grabbed for him.

Stockwell kicked the engine to life and cranked the throttle. Unmuffled, the small engine filled the room with a tinny bass that sent the mob reaching for their ears. He dropped the bike on its side and hoped the weight of the vehicle would keep the grip twisted and throttle wide open.

Damian grabbed a third bike and rolled it onto the rail. Hands were upon him when he gunned the engine and shot down the track after Bertrand.

The design of the vehicle was stupidly ingenious. The rims sat the motorcycle firmly on the rail and the outrigger kept it balanced. Speed was its only limitation. To the right, Stockwell could lean into the turns as the outrigger lifted into the air. But, to the left, he was forced to slow and turn with the handlebars as the outrigger fought against him. For the purposes of discretely moving illicit gold mined by brainwashed slave labor, this was fine, but it made the bike impractical as a getaway vehicle.

He risked a glance behind him on each straight stretch of track. It had not taken the mob long to overcome the sound of the muffler. There were several motorcycles behind him. Each had a single rider and another man standing on the outrigger.

Stockwell smirked; they wouldn't be able to catch him. Twice the riders placed twice the burden on the small engines. As a single rider, he would be able to outrun them indefinitely. He rounded a bend in the track. "Dammit, Bertrand."

The whine of the engine told Stockwell that the cycle ahead of him was at full throttle, but with Simmons in tow and the ore cart forcing the Frenchman to steer with only the handlebars, the vehicle was moving too slow. Damian caught up quickly.

"Move."

Bertrand threw a vicious glance over his shoulder. "It is doing all the moving it can do! It is a stupid machine."

Stockwell looked back over his shoulder. The masked men were gaining.

"Bertrand, is there anything you can do?"

"I could leave you and your friend here."

It wasn't like his friend to get all testy. "Take it easy, Bertrand."

"Take it easy? I am brainwashed. You beat me up. We are dragged down here. We are shot at with spears and beat up. Then I walk a really long way in the jungle to save you and more people beat us up. We finally get to run and it is on this stupid thing. It is hot. I am sweaty and my hands hurt."

Stockwell shook his head and eased up on the gas. He fell closer to the pursuers but further from the whining. He looked around. Normally, he had an instinctive sense of location but the total darkness of the night before had robbed him of any landmarks. He didn't know where he was on the tracks. It all looked the same—trees, rails and vines.

Still, he thought, the spur line he had spotted couldn't be too far away. At first he thought it led to salvation for Simmons. Now he just wanted to get away from the whiny Frenchman.

It appeared suddenly. The spur line ran to the left and was swallowed by the jungle almost instantly. The junction switch, all but invisible the night before, was mounted at the crotch of the spur.

Damian stood and drew the massive Smith & Wesson. By his count, there were still three rounds remaining in its oversized cylinder. He took aim over the valet's head. Bertrand was still complaining and couldn't hear Stockwell's warning to duck.

The first shot boomed and struck the junction switch just before Bertrand reached the spur. The bike veered suddenly to the left and almost tossed the Frenchman into the jungle. He recovered quickly and continued to complain.

Stockwell fired again and set the track back in place just as his own vehicle hit the spur. With the Frenchman out of the way, he could speed up again and make haste to the plantation. He placed the weapon back in the sling and risked a glance to check the status of his pursuers.

It had been his experience that, almost 100% of the time, whenever a man was soaring through the air towards you with a cane knife, that the man would be screaming. It was always unnerving, but served as a nice warning should a man be flying at you with a cane knife. This masked warrior did not scream, but, still, he soared through the air wielding a cane knife.

The mob had caught up and the warrior leapt from the outrigger of the pursuer's bike onto Stockwell's. Though the man was silent, the knife whistled as it cut through the air. It was enough for Damian's reflexes to take over.

Damian pulled his hand from the throttle and caught the warrior's wrist. The blade stopped just above the bridge of his nose. The strength of the masked man was tremendous. Stockwell felt his massive muscles quiver as he fought to keep the large, flat blade out of his head. It moved closer.

The sudden lack of throttle caused the bike to slow dramatically. The masked rider rammed into him from behind. The rims meshed and twisted together. Stockwell's rear wheel lifted from the track, threw the weight of the knife-wielding attacker forward over the gas tank and forced Damian to let go of the handlebars.

Behind him, the front wheel lifted from the track and slammed back to the ground. It missed the rail, dug into the ground between the spurs and sent the bike flying end over end into the jungle.

Stockwell's bike pitched to the right, the outrigger rose into the air as the extra weight of the masked man slumped over his gas tank threatened to spill them from the tracks. Damian stood and threw the bike to the left. The outrigger sparked as it slammed back onto the rail.

The momentum carried the warrior back into the armature and Stockwell grabbed the handlebars.

Unfazed, the masked man swung the cane knife at Stockwell's leg.

Damian leapt as the blade arced toward him. His powerful legs carried him from the seat of the bike and into the air—his grip ever firm on the handle bars, his body peaked parallel to the ground. For a moment it felt as if he was flying.

The blade sunk deep into the leather seat as Stockwell brought his feet back down, first on the hand that held the knife and then on the chest of his attacker.

The masked warrior lost his purchase on the blade and fell deeper into the wireframe outrigger.

Before his attacker could recover, Damian pulled the knife from the seat and struck at the man's head. The cut was precise. The cane knife nicked only the top corner of the mask. Green mist began to spout from the horrid face. Stockwell dropped the knife and grabbed the warrior by his hair. As the acid sprayed from the corner of the mask, Damian forced the stream into the bars of the outrigger. The powerful acid ate away at the metal and, with a barely audible "chink," each brace separated from the bike. The outrigger and the masked warrior fell away.

Free of the restrictive armature, Stockwell gunned the throttle and pulled away from the other pursuers. He leaned into every left and right curve—never touching the brakes. Every bend in the track allowed him to increase his lead over the chase vehicles that were still restricted by the outriggers.

Confined to the rails, however, he would never be able to lose them. He had spotted no other spur lines on the walk in and the rail lines were fairly set in their paths. No, they couldn't be shaken. They would have to be stopped. With only one bullet left in the Smith & Wesson, he would have to think of something other than just plain shooting them.

Stockwell grinned and leaned forward over the handlebars. He knew what to do.

The green mesh of the jungle blurred in his peripheral as he focused on the tracks ahead. He made considerable ground without the cumbersome outrigger to slow him down. His keen eyes scanned the track ahead and the wall of green beside him for any clue to his location. The darkness of the night had revealed few landmarks, but as he rode he noticed the non-visual markers he had picked up during his run: the scent that hung in the air was rich with vegetation, that which grew and that which rotted on the jungle floor, the tapestry of sounds that came from beyond the walls of green had changed its song during the day as a new chorus of insects and creatures took over for the nocturnal hunters.

There began a series of slight rises and falls in the track. That they had been laid so well in the thickest of jungles was a remarkable feat of engineering, but even hypnotized slave labor had issues with grading occasionally. As the bike began to bounce, he lay off the gas and slowed. He knew where he was.

The gains he had made were not as significant as he had assumed. While the presence of the second rider was a burden on the small cycles' engines, the added weight on the outrigger had enabled his hunters to corner without slowing. It was only a moment before the remaining two bikes were in sight. He needed them close.

Stockwell smiled and twisted the throttle. The metal rim spun on the track, caught and shot the bike forward. He gained speed and rounded a slight bend as the masked men behind him gained. Yes, this was the place.

Damian drew the Smith & Wesson from the sling on his back and fired the remaining round into the jungle. The slug struck the crotch of a tree and shattered the bark. The sound woke the jaguar.

Stockwell holstered the gun and shot past the giant cat as it leapt onto the tracks—irritable and hungry. Rage filled the creature's face as Stockwell continued down the track and out of sight. The savage beast turned toward the approaching cycles.

The influence of the mask shielded the men from the danger in front of them. They held fast the throttles and roared down the track with no regard for the two-hundred-pound killer in their path.

The silken black cat crouched low to the rails and sprang. Its weight pulled the rider from the first bike and drove him to the tracks. Without a pilot, the motorcycle swayed out of control and toppled over, taking the masked man on the outrigger to the ground.

Following close at full speed, the second bike plowed into the fallen man and flipped through the air as the back end sped over the front. A moment later, all four men lay across the rail line unable to move.

The jaguar bit into the first man's face and roared in pain as the green gas seeped from the puncture marks. The mighty predator writhed in pain and bolted into the jungle, pawing at its face as it went. Its cries of anguish filled the jungle and silenced the other beasts.

Stockwell looked up from the rearview mirror. There was nothing behind him now. All of the trouble lay ahead.

# 22

## End of the Line

The rail line ended suddenly. There was no terminus, no end of the line signage—the rails simply stopped. Stockwell leapt from the bike as the rims left the rail and ran into a wall of vegetation. The bike crashed through the brush and into a clearing. The tracks had led him right to the plantation.

Damian ducked through the hole made by the rail-bike, crouched in the bushes and peered into the courtyard. The way Zippy had spoken, the mad god's men would already be on the grounds. He would have to be cautious. Trained killers were dangerous enough, but under the influence of the masks they could be deadly—even to him.

There was little movement on the grounds. There were no other bikes near the rail line. Perhaps he had beaten the masked men here. It was possible. It wouldn't surprise him in the least if the despotic god that had forced men into slave labor via hypnotic control was also a brazen liar.

He listened. There were no voices. There was no banter among men that was so common in the fraternal atmosphere that mercenary armies created.

From the cover of the jungle he saw nothing out of the ordinary. Still, he approached with caution. From the multiple encounters of assailants, it was clear that the mask enhanced the abilities of the men it possessed. Workers from the field had an endurance that was inhuman, but their fighting skills were lacking. Bertrand, however, had become a fierce opponent under its influence. The science of the mask increased his reflexes, strength and pain threshold. Imagining Dalton's well-trained security force under the power of the mask gave him pause. Each would be a formidable foe and together the army would be unstoppable.

Damian rolled from the jungle and across the clearing to the cover of a tree. Scanning the main house, he saw only empty balconies. The residence doors were open and unguarded. He had not spent enough time at the plantation the previous day to learn the guards' patterns or observe their security methods, but he knew that a complete lack of presence was a bad sign.

He dashed from the tree to the edge of the home and vaulted onto the porch. Settling with his back against the wall, he edged toward to an open window. There was no sound from inside the home. It felt deserted.

At this time of day the plantation should be abuzz with workers. Even the executives would be moving about as the crops were harvested and sent to port. Damian stepped over the sill and through the window in the drawing room.

The room was well appointed and empty. He chuckled that, even a hemisphere away, floral prints dominated the furniture. Despite his extensive studies on the working of the human mind, there was no clear reason why people preferred to sit on pictures of flowers when, while out in nature, no person ever saw a patch of flowers and suddenly said, "I must sit on those. They look comfortable."

He held still for a full minute and listened to the home. Nothing creaked. Nothing slammed. There was no breath to the house. He was alone.

He moved silently into the hall. By keeping close to the wall, he ensured that his own weight would not trigger any creaks hidden in the wooden floor. Though he moved quietly, he moved quickly throughout the first floor. The residence and the offices were deserted. There was little doubt in his magnificent mind that Zipacna's men had reached the plantation first. A well-trained army was now under the mad god's control. Stockwell sighed, "I'm going to need more bullets."

His room was on the second floor and he trusted that his bags had been delivered as Dalton had promised. Caution preceded every footstep as he moved up the stairs. Even keeping his weight at the outer edge of the steps betrayed his presence with a minor creak. The humidity played havoc with the wood flooring here. Constant expansion and contraction made every floorboard an alarm for the vigilant man. He slowed his pace and listened intently to sounds of the second floor.

Like the one below it, there was nothing. Through a series of daily exercises and sensory deprivation, he had trained his hearing to be more keen than the average man. But, even his own delicate senses could detect no one on the second floor.

Zipacna would most likely rally his new minions to the mine. Especially now that Bertrand and Simmons were on their way to the authorities. The Mayan was left with few options. Since he did not actually possess the power to envelop the temple within the Earth's crust as he claimed, he would either abandon the mine or prepare to defend it from whatever forces the Honduran government would send.

Several encounters with mad gods had taught Stockwell that it would be the latter. It took a massive ego to adopt the persona of a god. And, while hubris alone would demand it, the added elements of gold fever and an army of mindless yet loyal minions would ensure that Zipacna would fight to the last man rather than abandon his greed-driven efforts.

Damian stepped onto the landing, made his way to his room and entered with caution. It was empty but for his luggage. The bags had been delivered to the room and set on a small chest at the foot of the bed. He opened a leather satchel and selected a box of ammunition. He pulled the Smith & Wesson from the sling, swung out the cylinder and emptied the brass into his palm. He tossed the spent casings onto the bed and opened the box labeled "hot." The rounds inside were custom loaded for higher velocity but would also give him a bigger bang and, as sonic assaults seemed to be the best weapon against the control of the mask, the bigger the bang, the better.

He had placed one round in the chamber when he heard the squeak of a neglected hinge behind him. With one move he raked his palm against the cylinder and sent it spinning, snapped his wrist and spun around, shutting the cylinder with the round in place before the hammer.

The mask was the same as all the others, but the massive body behind it could only belong to Humberto. The large Honduran charged from the closet and grabbed the revolver by the barrel before Stockwell could bring it to bear on his target. Humberto forced the barrel towards the ground.

The head of security's grip was fierce and threatened to wrench the gun from Damian's hand. Stockwell pulled the trigger. The hand-loaded round was deafening in the small room and the report dulled his own hearing as the world around him became a roar.

Humberto winced and released the barrel. The massive guard grabbed at his hand.

Stockwell paused. It was not the sound of the report but the heat of the barrel that had caused the guard to withdraw. But that meant ...

Humberto recovered quickly and swung a melon-sized fist at Stockwell.

Damian brought his arm up to catch the blow. It saved him from taking a strike to the head, but the force knocked him over the bed and across the room. He let the empty weapon fall to the ground and turned to face the guard.

Humberto placed one hand under the bed and threw it out of his way and charged.

Damian stepped to one side and directed the massive man into the wall. The impact caused the room to shake as Humberto continued through the wallboard. Stockwell brought his fist down on the back of the man's neck.

The goliath let out a groan and pulled himself from the wall.

"That's enough, Humberto."

The horrid face of the mask looked blankly back at him. One of the soulless glass eyes had shattered upon impact with the wall. Humberto's own brown eye stared back at Stockwell. It seemed to be smiling.

The giant man lunged and caught Stockwell around the waist. His massive arms locked together as he continued the charge.

"I said that's enough ..."

The powerful legs picked Stockwell up from the ground and drove him towards the room's exterior wall. Both men crashed through the window and to the ground below.

The fall was bad enough, but the large man landing on top of him did little to keep the air in Stockwell's lungs. This made explaining that he knew what was happening difficult. He was on to the guard, but couldn't tell him.

Humberto recovered first and picked Stockwell from the ground. For all of his life, Damian had been a big man. His god given height and the hard-earned build of an Olympian had prepared him for many things, but being thrown across the grounds of a banana plantation by a giant named Humberto was not one of them. He landed hard on his back and slid another foot before the force of the guard's throw waned. Stockwell rolled to his feet and struggled to catch his breath.

The monster was upon him. Stockwell dodged another tackle and countered with a knee to the man's chest.

Humberto stood and unleashed a fury of punches, but the man was a grappler and Stockwell easily dodged the awkward blows.

Damian countered and landed several strikes of his own. He was forced to work the body as every strike to the mask tore at his knuckles. He threw furiously and felt several of Humberto's ribs crack, but the damage did little to slow the guard down. With each strike he heard the man react.

"I can hear you in there, Humberto. Not one man has made a sound through that mask when I beat on them. Not one. But you whine. You wheeze. You're in there."

A lucky left caught Stockwell on the cheek and sent him reeling across the lawn into a tree. It had felt more like a force of nature than a man's blow. Damian spit blood and stared at the man. "Take it off, Humberto. Let's do this face-to-face."

Humberto stood up straight and lifted his hand to the mask. He pulled it free. No gas hissed. No acid consumed the horrid face. Humberto dropped the mask to the ground and smiled.

Stockwell smiled back, "There you are, Zippy."

Humberto rushed. Stockwell charged. The two giants met in the open grounds of the plantation. Stockwell ducked a right and drove his fist into the now unprotected face of the massive Honduran.

Humberto reeled back and Stockwell followed through with a second strike to the head as he sidestepped a counter punch. Damian stepped inside a grasp and worked the broken ribs with three quick blows.

Humberto grabbed Stockwell by the shoulders and drove his head forward.

Stockwell lowered his face and let the hardest part of his head meet the guard's nose.

Each skull rattled.

Humberto picked Stockwell up from the ground and threw him against the tree.

He did not collapse to the ground but stood dazed with the tree supporting his weight.

Humberto punched for his head.

Stockwell dropped to the ground and heard the man's hand break as it met the wood of the tree. He struck at Humberto's knee and dropped the guard to the ground. Damian leapt over the guard and locked his arm around the man's throat. His intent was not to kill, but as the Honduran struggled against the hold, he began to wonder if the man would give him a choice.

Humberto tried to stand but could not. He used his good hand to keep himself from the ground and wrapped the other around Stockwell's forearm, struggling to pull it from his windpipe. But the broken hand no longer had the strength.

Stockwell could feel the consciousness fading from Humberto's body as his lungs struggled to draw oxygen that wasn't there. The strongest man Stockwell had ever faced went limp and collapsed beneath him.

Stockwell stood and looked down at the large Honduran. "And thus falls the mad Mayan god Zipacan ... Zipan ... Zippy."

The crack of gunshots filled the grounds as dirt began to burst at his feet. The fertile plantation soil erupted into plumes of dust all around him. Stockwell crouched low and sprinted for cover. Masked men were everywhere and closing in around him. They emerged from the warehouse and sheds around the property. They poured from the jungle wall at the plantation's perimeter. They had him surrounded.

These men weren't dressed in loincloths and threadbare worker's garments. Each wore the uniform of the All-American Banana Company and brandished a rifle.

Damian vaulted the rail of the porch and dove through an open window into the home. He scrambled on all fours across the floor as chunks of plaster, wood and other building materials exploded around him. Zipacna had his army.

The hail of bullets was continuous. Damian scrambled to the doorway and leapt into the hall. He slid across the polished wood floor and slammed into the wall. The bullets found him there as well. The walls of the home were not enough to stop the high-powered rifles. His best chance of escape was out the back door. He stayed low and crawled quickly to the end of the hall. Before he could break for the back door, he heard the front crash from its hinges. Two masked guards rushed into the home. The soulless black eyes spotted Stockwell on the floor and each guard brought their rifle to bear on the helpless man.

Damian was on his feet before the front door collapsed to the ground. Seizing the barrel of the closest rifle in his left hand, he pulled the guard off balance and drove his elbow through the mask.

The guard screamed as splinters of the shattered veneer burst into his face. Still, there was no mist.

Stockwell tore the rifle from the guard's grip and shoved the stock into the next guard's face. The mercenary fell to the ground unconscious. Blood ran from under the mask, but still, it remained intact.

Damian bent down and pulled the mask from the guard's face and examined its interior. Unlike the masks he had found in the mine, this one was devoid of any circuitry. It was simply a mask. It held no special power over the men at the plantation. They were acting of their own free will. "Dammit."

Stockwell dropped the rifle and stepped out onto the porch. He stood and screamed over the sound of the gunfire. "Dalton! Show yourself!"

Men continued to pour from various buildings of the compound. The shots had stopped, but the men closed in. Stockwell made no move to run.

"Show yourself, Dalton!"

More than twenty men converged on the porch, rifles pointed squarely at Stockwell's chest. They couldn't miss from this range.

"Now, Cole!"

At the edge of the grounds, the jungle parted. Zipacna emerged from the curtain of vegetation that hid the rail line from site. The Mayan god did not move with haste but covered the open space quickly with long strides. The group of soldiers parted as the massive cloaked figure reached the home and stepped onto the porch.

The enormous figure leaned in. The horrid mask was inches from Stockwell's face. Like steam from a rusted pipe, his voice spit from the carved image. "The mighty Stockwell. You're captured all too easy."

Stockwell spoke into the chest of the Mayan god. "Lose the getup, Dalton, I know it's you."

Zipacna chuckled the same grating laugh from the cave as he reached up and grabbed the medallion that held the cloak closed across his chest. He loosened the clasp and pulled the cloak free. He then grabbed the mask and removed it. The cloak fell to the ground and Cole Dalton stared his old friend in the eyes.

"I knew it was you."

"You thought it was Humberto."

"I did not."

"You did too. I was hiding in the bushes and I heard you say that you had defeated Zipacna. Now you know that's not ..."

"I didn't say that. "

"What? Yes you did. I heard you."

"I never said I defeated Zipacna."

"Maybe not those exact words but it was ..."

"I thought you said you heard me. Obviously you're lying."

Cole tucked the mask under one arm and pointed to the jungle. "Right there, Dam. I was right there. You thought that Humberto was Zipacna."

"Did not."

Dalton sighed, "Fine, you know what? It doesn't matter. We've got you and it just doesn't matter."

"How could you, Dalton? How could you do this?"

"The science isn't as tricky as you'd think. It's ..."

"I don't mean that. How could you create an army of mindless slaves? How could you take God's greatest gift to man and twist it to your own selfish means? How could you betray the gift of free will and liberty? Something you and I have fought all our lives to protect."

"Dam, you're such a fool. Free will isn't the greatest gift. God's greatest gift to man was other men and that is not at all how I meant that to sound. Free will is an illusion. Money. Power. These are the only things the world understands."

"But, you had all that. What of your yellow gold?"

"Real gold is so much better. I am so sick and tired of these damn bananas. And these bugs and this humidity. My fortune lies in Zipacna's temple, not the trees of this godforsaken country."

Stockwell shook his head. "Of all the men I've known, you were the last I would have suspected to turn to a life of nefarious deeds."

Dalton's brow creased, "It's easy for you. Born rich. Had you struggled like I have, you would have seized the same opportunity."

"I value freedom more than gold, old friend."

"Then you are a fool."

Damian couldn't believe Dalton had turned so evil. The man's character was too strong. There had to be some other explanation. "You've been away too long, my friend. You've forgotten the beauty of freedom. You need to come home. Then you'll remember."

Dalton smirked. He placed the mask back on his head. The raspy voice, filtered through some mechanical device, returned. "I'll be back soon enough. You'll be staying here."

Zipacna turned and moved back through the crowd.

"I'm sorry, my friend. I'm going to have to stop you."

Zipacna paused. He turned back to the mighty adventurer. "Stop me? I'm the one with the army." He turned away and stepped through the crowd.

Stockwell felt a stinging in his neck. The sharp pain appeared suddenly in multiple places across his back. The pain turned to numbness as he fell to his knees. He caught himself with one hand but the effort lasted only a moment as the rest of his body went numb and he collapsed to the ground.

# 23

## The End of Another Line

Before he opened his eyes, he knew he was back in the cavern. The acrid smell of the acid eating away at the rocks was enough to tell him where he was. He could clearly hear the hissing as the chemical struck the rock walls. This also told him his hearing had returned to normal. He must have been out for hours for his ears to recover from the gunshot.

He wasn't on the ground. His feet dangled beneath him. This fact, combined with the bindings on his hands, told him his precise location. Stockwell opened his eyes and looked down. "Yep. Big tub of acid."

The massive cauldron in the center of the cavern bubbled and steamed with the green chemical he had come to despise over the last few days. His bare feet were but ten feet above the corrosive mixture. His shirt had been stripped away as well. Dalton knew too well the host of gadgets he kept in his garments and had no doubt seen to their removal. A glance up confirmed what he had known. Rope bound his hands and suspended him from the boom arm of a crane. Fatigue in his shoulders indicated that he had been there for a while.

"Dam, you sure can sleep." Cole Dalton climbed a ladder to the control cabin of the crane. "Although, my men may have over done it with the darts."

"Only a coward shoots a man in the back."

"Spare me your code of honor, Dam. As you can see, I've kind of let noble and good deeds go."

Stockwell scanned the cavern. Dalton's army lined the perimeter of the cave, unmasked but armed. Possessed men toiled in the sweltering heat of the mine. The process was as brutal as it was efficient. Acid ate the rock. Gold fell. Men collected it and the process began again.

"What happened to you, Cole? What turned you toward evil?"

Dalton smiled and moved one of the levers. The boom shook and Stockwell began to sway as the crane moved back and forth over the vat.

"I almost killed you, you know. For three days I toyed with the idea. But, well, I just couldn't do it."

"Isn't that sweet." Three days? Had he been out for so long?

"I'm afraid not, old friend. You see, I really, really need you dead. As soon as Simmons turned up here, I knew you'd have to die. That's why I sent my man to New York."

"You should have come yourself."

"Oh, I was there. Who do you think bolted the mask to his face?"

Stockwell winced. He had seen horrific things done to men, but never by such a close ally. How could he have been so wrong about Dalton? Something must have changed the man.

"In all fairness, I tried to stop Simmons from coming here. I didn't want any of my friends to get hurt. But, you see, he'd discovered the same secret I had and he knew that the mine had to be real. There was no stopping him. Just like there will be no stopping me."

"Ah, my old friend. How many times have we been in this situation? Me, dangling perilously above certain death? Lava, sharp rocks, alligators, etcetera. The villain running at the mouth?"

"Plenty of times, Dam. And, I know what you're getting at. I realize that it's never worked out for the man at the controls. So, I've taken a few precautions." Dalton stepped from behind the control panel with Damian's shirt and boots in his hands. He held up the clothes. "Your magic bag. Chemicals, filaments, weapons, explosives. I've always admired your fashion sense, Dam."

Dalton tossed the articles in the acid. The boots splashed and sunk into the green liquid but the shirt drifted on top. Seconds later it blazed to life. Chemicals ignited. Smoke plumed as the different devices reacted with the acid. The different buttons popped and exploded to varying degrees and all became calm as the collar sank below the surface. A second later there was a massive boom and an eruption of acid.

"Whoa." Dalton laughed. "What was that last one?"

"The collar stays. They're dynamite."

"You are a remarkable man, my friend." Dalton stepped back behind the control panel. "So with that taken care of, let's start the questioning."

"Fine. What's your plan?"

"No. No, no. I'm asking the questions."

"I don't get to ask any?"

"What? No. Besides, I don't think there's really anything to clarify. If you look around, my plan is pretty obvious. Isn't it?"

"Certainly, but what's next? What do you plan to do with the gold?"

"Get rich." Dalton laughed. "I'm sorry, Dam. It's not really any more complicated than that."

"You've turned on your friends, on yourself, your very nature, for money?"

"Well, in my defense, it is a lot of money."

"I never imagined you to be so shallow."

Dalton shrugged. "I've got nothing but respect for you, Damian. I just want you to know that before I burn your feet off." Dalton moved a lever on the panel. The arm began to lower Stockwell towards the acid.

"You expect me to talk?"

"After a fair bit of screaming, yes."

"You'll get nothing out of me."

"Oh, I'm sure by the time we get to the knees you'll tell me what I want to know. Where's Bertrand? Where's Simmons?"

"He took the spur line and went to get the army." Stockwell smiled. That explained the heightened security. The Frenchman had succeeded in his escape. With any luck, he'd be returning with the Honduran military at any moment.

"Wow. You gave him up quick."

"It's just Bertrand."

"What about all that 'you'll get nothing out of me' nonsense?"

"I thought the question might be harder. Besides, knowing where he is won't stop him from kicking your teeth in."

"You sent him for help?"

"It's not my proudest moment."

"Well, then. I guess I was worried for nothing."

The boom continued its descent. Stockwell watched the acid draw nearer. "You own the authorities, don't you?"

"Every last one. I told you it was a lot of money. It buys a lot of friends." Dalton stepped away from the controls.

"Corrupt governments won't stop Bertrand. You know that."

"He is feisty. I'll give him that."

"He also understands loyalty and honor."

"Your bag of tricks is gone, so you're throwing insults? I expected more from you, Dam." Dalton descended the ladder to the ground.

"You're right. Insults are beneath me. Besides, I don't blame you for your lapse in judgment. I know what's happened to you and it's not your fault."

Dalton stopped and turned back to his captive. "Well, this is a new one. I've never seen you try to escape using reverse psychology."

"This is no trick, old friend. I'm sad for you. It's obvious you've lost your way. That you could so easily take control of men's minds, their free will ... you've forgotten the power of freedom. You've been gone too long."

"Freedom? Money is freedom. You should know this better than anyone."

"Money is a tool, Dalton. Nothing more. Freedom lies in men's hearts, in their souls. It manifests itself in great deeds of sacrifice and great places like America."

"America is a failed experiment. It's been laboring under its own failure since '29."

"You've been gone too long."

"I read the papers."

"Freedom's engine may have sputtered, but its spirit lives on."

"Ha. Spirit is nothing without force."

"I disagree. Sometimes the spirit is enough."

"You're a fool, Dam. A damned fool."

"A lot's changed since you've been gone, Cole. We even adopted a national anthem."

"Another distraction for the masses. In a way my mind control device is kinder."

Stockwell looked to the ceiling. The boom was lowering him to the exact center of the cavern. Damian drew a deep breath and sang. "O say, can you see?"

"Hrrrmph." Dalton turned his back on his old friend.

"By the dawn's early light."

"Sounds wonderful, Dam. I can't believe you've chosen this jingoistic nonsense to be your last words. I'll make sure and write them down."

"What so proudly we hailed at the twilight's last gleaming." The lyrics bounced off the cavern walls, building on themselves to tremendous volume.

Dalton stopped and turned back to the vat. "No!"

"Whose broad stripes and bright stars through the perilous fight ..."

The masked workers slowed in their labor. The boom dropped Stockwell lower. Dalton rushed back to the ladder.

"O'er the ramparts we watched, were so gallantly streaming?"

Dalton scrambled up the ladder, screaming to the guards, "Shoot him! Shoot him!"

But, it was too late. The crane's boom lowered Damian into the cavern's acoustical center. His baritone voice, perfect in pitch and tone, boomed louder than the Smith & Wesson and bounced from the rock surface to the delicate circuitry of Dalton's hideous masks.

"And the rockets' red glare, the bombs bursting in air ..."

The workers grabbed for their ears.

"Gave proof through the night that our flag was still there."

Sparks flew from the eyes of the masks. Everywhere, electrical snaps and the smell of ozone filled the air.

"O say, does that star-spangled banner yet wave ..."

Masks fell to the ground inert. Hundreds of men who had labored in a fog of servitude became self-aware for the first time in months. The guards became aware of what was happening and reached for their weapons. Dalton stumbled on the ladder in his haste.

"O'er the land of the free ..."

One of the guards drew a bead on Stockwell as he dangled from the boom. Several workers tackled him before he could fire.

Dalton found his footing and made the top of the platform. He dove for the control lever.

"And the home of the brave?"

Chaos erupted in the cavern as the freed mind-slaves set upon the security force. Shots were fired in futility as the swarm of captives rushed the guards.

Dalton shoved the lever forward and the boom dove towards the acid.

Damian flexed his mighty arms and he pulled himself up with such force that the bonds cleared the hook making it possible to grab the descending boom. He pulled himself on the beam and as the hook splashed into the vat, it began to dissolve. He raced up the boom and dove for the platform.

Dalton scrambled back and fell off the edge to the ground below.

Stockwell rolled to the edge of the scaffold and watched as Cole took to his feet and ran for the entrance of the cavern. Descending the ladder with his bound hands cost him precious seconds that Dalton exploited for a lead. This was something he would have to practice. It was a skill he would have to add to his training.

His bare feet hit the cavern floor and he rushed after his former friend, dodging frenzied workers and overwhelmed guards as he went. The captives were more than holding their own. One would assume that the forced labor had left them exhausted, but there was always strength in freedom.

One guard had gained the upper hand and was waving a pistol at a host of captives. The guard was frightened and screaming at the men to stay back. Damian rushed through the threatened crowd and burst out of the throng of men, diving at the guard.

He tackled the man at the waist and took him to the ground. The gun clattered into the cavern and Damian brought his bound fists down on the man's head. The blow left the guard unconscious.

Several hands began to pull at him and Stockwell turned to see the workers helping him to his feet. One of the men produced a knife and cut the rope that held his hands. They surrounded him and began to pat him on the back. A chorus of thank yous came from raspy voices that had not spoken in months.

Stockwell brushed off the appreciation and turned to see Dalton disappear through the tunnel to the surface. He started to pursue but a hand held him back. Damian turned back the crowd of workers, about to explain that he must catch Zipacna, when he saw why they had restrained him. One of the battered and tired hands produced the gun the guard had dropped and offered it to him.

It was the Smith & Wesson. Stockwell took the gun.

"Vas. Vas." The workers waved him on and Stockwell rushed into the tunnel towards the surface.

# 24

## Friends Like These

Gun drawn, anger peaked, Damian ran up the ancient tunnel towards the temple's entrance. As he ran, he dropped the cylinder of the Smith & Wesson and counted the rounds. The cylinder was full but in the brief glance he saw the indention from the firing pin in two of the cartridges. Stockwell snapped the cylinder back into place and rushed into the temple's alcove.

The hand that grabbed his face was callous, huge and smelled a bit. It gripped his head and pulled him forward to the ground while another equally large hand pulled the gun from his grasp.

Stockwell rolled across the floor and collided with the wall beneath the carving that depicted Zipacna exacting his vengeance on the world. Before he could stand, he felt the large hands grasp the waist of his pants. They lifted him from the ground. Neither his hands nor feet could make contact with the earth and he soon found himself soaring through the air as the powerful arms heaved him out the temple's entrance and into the fading daylight. Damian tumbled and rolled to his feet facing the temple.

Humberto's massive frame filled the entranceway as he stared hate into Damian's eyes. His left hand held the Smith & Wesson by the barrel but he made no move to use the weapon. The two were locked at the eyes, each waiting for the other to move.

A slow clap began to echo from the temple's alcove. The sharp sound was amplified by the stone construction and did not fade until Dalton stepped past the large Honduran and into the evening air. "That ... now that was something! I mean, wow! I'm not quite sure what happened in there, but it was amazing."

"Your slaves have been freed, Dalton. Freed by the power of America."

"You never cease to amaze me, Dam. I'll bet Carnegie Hall has never even seen a performance like that."

"Think again. I opened for the Stars and Stripes Jubilee last summer."

Dalton nodded, "Of course you did. But, I'm sorry to say that this, my friend, was your ..."

"You're going to say my farewell performance, aren't you? You villains are so predictable."

"No, I wasn't," Dalton stammered.

"Yes, you were."

"I wasn't going to say it. But, it was. That was your ..."

"Swan song?" Damian shook his head. "It's pathetic really. You'd think for all the villains you've encountered over the years, you'd have picked up some better rhetoric."

Dalton smiled. "Enough. It doesn't matter how I put it, this is the end of the great Damian Stockwell."

"How do you figure? There's an army of very angry, free men making their way from the mine. And it's just you and Humberto there to stop them."

Humberto lurched forward. Dalton stayed him with a raised hand. He smiled at Stockwell and signaled for him to turn around.

Damian looked over his shoulder. In the corner of his eye he saw a member of the banana company's security force with a rifle pointed at his back. He turned further and saw thirty men just like the first. "Oh. I didn't see those guys there."

Dalton signaled to the men and several of them rushed into the temple. Damian momentarily lost them in the shadows. Soon muzzle flashes and reports filled the alcove as the security force kept the freed workers pinned inside the mine.

"So, now that I've pointed out the army standing directly behind you, we'll have this conversation again."

"Okay. Do you want to say, 'it's curtains for me'?"

Dalton laughed, but there was no smile on his face. "Dam, I hope you know that I don't want to have you killed. I'm still going to do it, but you've always been a good friend. So, when I do have you killed, I want you to understand that it doesn't really change our friendship."

"It might a little. I know I'll like you less."

Dalton threw up his hands, "Why do you always have to be so good? If there was just a little evil in you, we could make this all work."

"Ha. Evil? Like you?"

"Yes! Exactly! If you could see things my way, we could stay friends, I wouldn't have to kill you and everything would be fine. Just like it was."

Stockwell looked at the security force behind him. Each had their rifle trained on his back. He looked back to Humberto—the brute was barely able to restrain his hatred. Finally, he looked at Dalton. His friend was being sincere. He had no desire to give the order to fire. He knew Cole desperately wanted him to say that everything would be fine, that they could continue to be friends. Damian valued friendship more than anything. Cole had travelled the seductive path of greed into a dark corner of his soul. Could he still be brought back? The man would have to answer for his crimes but he had seen many men turn from evil.

Stockwell looked his friend in the eye. He saw hope. Hope that he would say that it was all right to enslave men and force them to harvest riches from the earth for him, but he just couldn't. "Dalton. I'd like nothing more than to end this without bloodshed. I value our friendship more than you know. And, I'd like to see things your way, but I can't get my head that far up ..."

"Okay, just stop there." Dalton pulled the Smith & Wesson from Humberto's hand. "And you say I'm predictable."

"You're going to shoot me with my own gun? Some friend."

"Hardly." Dalton tossed the gun to the ground. "You see, since I'm about to have you killed, I'm going to need new friends." He put his hand on Humberto. "Humberto is my new friend and he very much would like to kill you with his bare hands. And, as his friend, I'm going to help him get what he wants."

"I'm afraid your new friend is going to be disappointed. I've already beaten him twice. The last time he kind of just went to sleep in the middle of our fight."

Humberto growled and balled his massive hands into fists.

"Oh, I know how tough you are, Dam. And, truth be told, you'd probably take Humberto a third time. But, he's my new friend and I want him to be happy. And, since you're not my friend anymore, I'm going to give him the gift I made for you." Dalton reached into his robe and pulled out a mask.

Stockwell had seen it before. It was the one Zipacna had tried to place on him earlier. Bulging eyes, a dangling tongue—Dalton placed the mask on Humberto's face. It was ridiculous.

"That's a good look for him."

"Make jokes. This mask is just like the others. Humberto is now stronger. His reflexes are faster. He feels no pain. And he is completely obedient to me. Whatever task I give him, he must accomplish. Humberto, kill Damian Stockwell."

Humberto rushed forward.

Stockwell backed away.

"Don't let him run, men. But, let Humberto have him."

The security force closed in around him and Damian was forced into Humberto's path.

The strikes came fast. Humberto was driven by powerful muscles and the circuitry of the mask. Damian found himself on the defensive as he dodged swing after swing. Humberto had been formidable during their first two encounters; now he was a mixture of rage and science that only a tank could take down.

What few lucky blows Stockwell landed were met with indifference and counterstrikes. As he rolled away, he scanned the surroundings hoping to play on the mask's one weakness—sound. But there was nothing but stone and jungle. Even a gunshot here would not have the same effect as in the cavern. The almost constant gunfire from the security guards in the alcove proved that. The air was too ... airy. The acoustics too poor. He would not be able to sing his way out of the fight.

Humberto landed a left fist to the side of his head. Stockwell fell to the ground and rolled as the security chief stomped the ground with his boot. The blow had caught him on the ear. His balance had not been affected, but a slight buzzing had appeared. It wasn't constant but it was frequent.

Footwork was a part of his daily training and he managed to avoid another direct hit. He sidestepped a right and landed his own on one of the mask's bulging eyes. Humberto was unfazed. Stockwell's fist hurt.

The buzzing grew louder and he began to notice that it wasn't just in his right ear. It had spread to both. Bugs? Had mosquitoes joined the fight against him as well? That wasn't fair.

Humberto's right hand shot out and grabbed Stockwell by the throat.

Damian grabbed the giant's wrist and tried to pry the hand away as fingers closed on his neck. He kicked at the massive man and caught him in the stomach.

Humberto did not flinch. With one arm, he lifted Stockwell from the ground.

Damian held fast to the man's forearm to prevent his own head from popping off. His feet dangled. He dug into the meat of Humberto's arm, simultaneously triggering two pressure points. It did nothing. That mask's effect was more powerful than the human nervous system.

Humberto began to squeeze.

Stockwell struggled to breathe. The buzzing grew louder and louder as his body began to scream out for air. He stared at the mask. Was this ridiculous face to be the last thing he saw? His vision began to blur. Darkness grew from the corners. The sound became louder. He dug deeper into Humberto's arm. There was still no response from the nerves. God, he needed air. He needed to breathe. What was that buzzing?

"What's that buzzing?" Dalton stared into the thick wall of the jungle trying to see beyond the leaves and vines. He heard the sound as well.

Stockwell, fighting to stay conscious for a moment more, smiled into the ridiculous mask and tried to speak. He could only mouth the word, Bertrand.

# 25

## Is This the End?

The bush cutter fell three trees as it emerged from the jungle wall. Each crashed in the clearing. Several of the security guards disappeared in the foliage as the others scrambled for safety. Two were caught in the spinning blades of the bush cutter.

Whatever damage the fire had done to the vehicle had been repaired. Even the outer hull of the tank-like equipment looked untouched. Williams had delivered against all odds. Even covered in blood, the machine was beautiful.

Saw blades cut into the air from all corners of the bush cutter and even as the security team recovered, they hesitated to approach it.

Stockwell, on the brink of unconsciousness, made one last effort to free himself from Humberto's iron grip. Summoning his waning strength he pulled his legs up and wrapped them around the brute's forearm. He pulled his knees to his chest and centered his mass around Humberto's hand.

Strength, reflexes—no amount of augmentation could overcome balance. Stockwell's weight pulled the masked guard forward and Damian fell to the ground with his neck still locked in Humberto's grip.

The large Honduran toppled forward.

Stockwell placed his feet on Humberto's ribs and, as the pair hit the ground, he kicked up, sending the guard flying over him.

Damian gasped for air as the hand was wrenched from his neck. Coughing, he struggled to all fours and breathed the humid jungle air deep into his lungs. He stood and stumbled. His balance was off but his vision returned as he got to his feet.

Unfazed by the fall, Humberto was already standing. The giant of a man stepped forward to fulfill his orders.

Damian backed into his defensive stance. He wobbled. "Damn you, equilibrium."

Bullets filled the air as the security force opened fire on the bush cutter. The shots produced only sparks as the rounds bounced off the heavy metal skin and turned into deadly ricochets. Despite their futility, the guards continued to fire until their rifles were empty.

Humberto rushed forward, beating the earth into dust as he closed the distance to Stockwell.

Damian braced himself.

Humberto pulled his right arm back to strike.

Two metallic clangs filled the air and Humberto jerked to his left and fell to the ground.

Stockwell turned to see Bertrand climbing from a hatch on top of the bush cutter with a smoking gun in his bare and bloodied hand. Williams was standing in the hatch next to him. The outfitter smiled, "Dam, you have the worst luck with clothes."

Bertrand dropped to the ground and rushed to Damian's side.

"Good man, Bertrand."

"Heads up!" Williams shouted and dropped into the bush cutter as more bullets splashed against its armor.

Bertrand and Stockwell dove for cover. "The temple! There are more guards inside."

The bush cutter lurched forward until its front end filled the entranceway. There was a massive flash as flamethrowers, installed for clearing vines, filled the alcove. Smoke rolled from the top of the entrance as the vehicle backed away. The hatch popped open and Williams stuck his head out. "Easy. The way you vagabonds always go on, you'd think this adventuring stuff would be difficult."

Stockwell laughed. "There'll be more men coming out. But they're the good guys."

"So. Don't burn 'em?"

"Right, don't burn 'em."

Williams backed the bush cutter away from the temple. Within moments the freed men rushed from the cavern and set up on the remaining guards.

"Monsieur. What has happened?"

"The slaves have been freed and Dalton has been defeated."

"Dalton?"

"Oh right, you didn't know. Dalton was Zippy."

"I cannot believe that."

"I didn't want to believe it either, but as you can see he's clearly wearing the costume." Stockwell pointed to the empty space where Dalton had stood. "Well crap. He ran away."

Damian raced to the temple entrance and searched the ground for any sign of a trail. The Smith & Wesson lay where Dalton had dropped it. Stockwell picked up the gun and raced into the jungle following a faint trail of footsteps left by his former friend.

Williams sat perched on the bush cutter watching the miners capture, but mostly beat, the remaining security force. "Shouldn't you go with him, Bertie?"

Bertrand shook his French head. "Non. This is something he has to do alone."

"He might need help."

"He can handle Monsieur Dalton."

"What about the big guy?"

Bertrand looked to where the giant masked guard had fallen. He was gone.

"Merde." Bertrand rushed after Stockwell.

The evening light filtered through the upper canopy and turned the jungle floor into a patchwork of shadows. The trail had all but disappeared in the dim light and Damian listened intently to the sounds of the jungle. The presence of a man would cause the animals and insects hesitation, so he listened for silence. It wasn't easy to hear silence with so much noise, but Stockwell was able to seek the quietest path as he moved cautiously through the dense vegetation.

He often trained barefoot to toughen his soles, but still the floor of the rainforest pricked at his feet and caused him to stumble. What felt like a thousand bugs landed on his bare chest and back. He could feel them nesting in his ample chest hair, but still he pushed on. Dalton had crossed over to madness. That much was clear. Whether it was his plan, gold fever or the damn bugs, something had driven him to the point of villainy. Damian had to pull him back from that point.

A limb cracked ahead and he increased his speed. He hoped the breeze generated by his quickened pace would motivate the bugs to leave, but he just kept running into more. He opened his mouth to curse them and swallowed three.

He spit out the bits that he didn't swallow and continued to listen for another sign of his old friend.

Stockwell followed the silence for fifteen minutes. The light grew dimmer and the chorus of the creatures changed as the nighttime pests took over. Soon the silence he chased was replaced by the faint roar of rushing water. A river could afford Dalton his escape. Stockwell moved faster until the roar was almost all he could hear.

Blind steps moved him forward now. He couldn't see the ground beneath his feet; he simply trusted that it would be there as he carried on. Suddenly, the ground wasn't there. Falling, he turned and grabbed a handful of earth and vine to stop his plummet. Looking over his shoulder, he could see the river a hundred feet below.

He pulled himself from the edge of the chasm back into the safety of the jungle and peered across the divide. There was no way he could jump it. There was no fallen log or rope bridge across it. Dalton was trapped on this side of the river.

"Dalton! Come out and let's talk about this."

Only silence responded. Silence and bugs.

"Your operations are ruined. Your slaves are freed. It's over."

The hissing voice of Zipacna seeped from the jungle. Its weakness made it difficult to pinpoint its origin. "I'll start over."

"I hate that voice, Dalton."

"I'm a little sick of yours as well, Damian."

Stockwell moved beneath the trees searching the darkness for his friend.

"Cole, we can work this out. Sure, there'll be jail time but I can see to it that you get sent to one of the less rapey prisons."

"There is no Cole Dalton. Not anymore. You've seen to that. You've practically killed me. But there is still Zipacna."

Damian looked to the branches. The sound of his voice drifted down from above.

"I will reclaim my mine. My workers. My fortune."

"I don't think so, Zippy."

"It won't be so difficult, once I kill you."

"That's not going to happen."

"Oh, but it is."

"Purely for argument's sake, and we're talking extremely hypothetical here, let's say you did kill me. People would come looking for me and they'd find you."

"Not here. The jungle is thick enough to swallow you and your legend."

"Now you're just being silly."

"The great Damian Stockwell—killed by a god," Zipacna hissed. The sound filled the jungle and grew louder until it consumed the canopy. Birds scattered. Limbs shook with scared monkeys.

There was a crashing to Damian's right. He drew the Smith & Wesson as Humberto burst from the jungle. The wound in his shoulder bled heavily and was covered with insects. He spotted Stockwell through the soulless eyes of the mask and charged.

Zipacna's hiss turned into a shriek as Dalton leapt from a tree limb. He dove at his former friend. In his hand was an ancient dagger that had been honed to a fine modern edge.

Humberto's orders were to kill Stockwell and Damian knew that he would drive them both over the cliff if it meant fulfilling that command. Shooting him would spare the fall but get him stabbed in the process.

Time slowed as he considered his options.

Humberto was too close. Shooting him now would still result in a collision and perilous fall to the river below.

In the darkness, Stockwell saw a flash of movement. He dropped to one knee and turned the gun towards Dalton.

Bertrand's foot struck from the jungle and impacted the side of Humberto's head. The strike pushed the giant Honduran off course and dislodged the mask from his face. The goofy expression flew through the air. Humberto ran into a tree.

"I'm sorry, my friend." Stockwell pulled the trigger on the .357 and placed a bullet though the grin of the mask. Green mist exploded from the hollow mask and created a cloud of acid in Dalton's path. The villain passed through the cloud face first and began to scream. He struck the ground and grabbed for his face.

Stockwell rushed to his friend's side and placed a hand on his shoulder.

"Cole, it's going ..."

Dalton screamed and looked into the eyes of his oldest friend.

"Whoa, that's gross." The green acid ate away at Cole's features and stripped him of his humanity. "Well, we'll ... um ... we'll get you to a doctor."

Writhing in pain, Dalton struggled to his feet.

"Dalton, sit down."

Cole clawed at the pain but only succeeded in stripping more flesh from his face. He stumbled along the edge of the chasm.

"Dalton, watch out for the edge."

Dalton slipped and fell from the edge of the jungle. He screamed as he plummeted to the river below.

Bertrand arrived at Stockwell's side and the pair peered over into the river. There was no sign of Dalton. Only Zipacna's robe could be seen dangling from a root that stretched into the chasm from the cliff.

"Dammit." Stockwell scanned the river for any sign of his friend. "I had just said watch out for the edge. I mean, I had just said it."

Bertrand nodded.

"You heard me, right, Bertrand?"

"Oui, I heard you."

"And, I heard me." Stockwell looked back into the chasm. "How did he not hear me?"

Humberto stood. His face was bloodied from the impact with the tree.

Stockwell turned to him. "Humberto, did you hear me say it?"

The giant Honduran roared and clenched his fists.

Stockwell shot him and looked back to the river below. The great adventurer shook his head and turned away. The sun had set and the moonlight did not extend beyond the edge of the chasm. The jungle was cast in absolute darkness.

"There's nothing we can do now. We should head back."

"Oui, Monsieur."

"Did you grab a flashlight?"

"Non, Monsieur."

"That's just sloppy, Bertrand."

# 26

## No, This is the End.

"You are very quiet, Monsieur." Stockwell was at the controls of the *Dahlia*. He had been lost in his own thoughts for hours. "I guess I am, Bertrand. If you want to turn in, you can. I've got this."

"Non, Monsieur. I don't feel like sleeping."

"You don't have to worry about me nodding off. Williams's snoring will keep me up."

The Vagabond Club's outfitter was draped over one of the passenger chairs in the cabin and had been snoring for hours.

"I don't think I could sleep either, Monsieur."

"Have it your way."

The silence returned.

"Monsieur if you need to talk, I'm ..."

"There's nothing really to talk about, Bertrand. Simmons regained his faculty and is overseeing the mining operation as the new head of the All-American Banana and Gold Company. The enslaved workers have all received a stake in the mine. And some big cat ate Humberto's corpse. The horror in Honduras has been stopped. All that's left is to get home to New York and enjoy the lack of bugs."

Bertrand had been with Damian for years. The great adventurer was a master of many things. He had overcome many horrors and defeated many foes, but Bertrand had never seen him like this. He knew that Stockwell had taken many lives, and that each one weighed on him. But, to have to kill a friend as close as Cole Dalton—he could not imagine how that tore at his soul.

Stockwell stared into the night beyond the windshield with a glare Bertrand had never seen. It was as if he was trying to stare down the world itself. The man was such a great amalgamation of strength, mind and imagination—each of humanity's greatest qualities was amplified in him. Bertrand could only imagine the fierceness of his regret and what Dalton's death had wrought upon him.

Dalton's body had never been found. Stockwell led the search efforts himself, enduring weeks in the sweltering heat and bug infested jungles that he so despised. There had been no trace of the man Stockwell had called his friend.

Bertrand wanted to say something, but there were no words. Not in his own language or in English that would stop the hurt he must be feeling. He simply stood and placed a bandaged hand on his good friend's shoulder.

Stockwell did not move. He did not take his eyes from the darkness before them.

Bertrand spoke quietly, "Bon nuit, Monsieur."

Stockwell nodded.

Bertrand moved into the cabin, fell into the passenger seat and closed his eyes.

# THE END

## Post-Apocalyptic Nomadic Warriors:
## A Duck & Cover Adventure

The post-apocalyptic world isn't that bad. Sure, there are mutants. But, for the people of New Hope, daily life isn't so much a struggle of finding food or medicine as it is trying to find a new shortstop for their kickball team.

This makes it difficult for a post-apocalyptic warrior to find work. Thankfully, an army full of killers is making its way to the peaceful town and plans to raze it to the ground. Only a fully trained post-apocalyptic-nomadic warrior can stop them.

Two have offered their services. One is invited to help. The other is sent to roam the wasteland. Did the townspeople make the right decision? Will they be saved? Did they find a shortstop? What's with all the bears?

Find out in *Post-Apocalyptic Nomadic Warriors*, a fast-paced action and adventure novel set in a horrific future that doesn't take itself too seriously.

# Tortugas Rising

Action, adventure, private islands, beautiful women, rhinos, boat chases, castles, car chases, fine dining, eco-terrorists, Savage man, The Rainbow Connection, a fortune, a father, dirty limericks, and two of the worst heroes ever to get caught up in a plot that could change the world forever.

Steve Bennett never knew his father. Now he's inherited a billion dollar empire and a stake in a man-made island chain in the Gulf of Mexico. Trying to adjust to his new situation, he and his best friend, Paul Nelson, travel to the islands and soon find themselves being chased by killers, killer hippies and rhinos. They have no training. They can't trust anyone. But, they must escape and stop a plot that threatens America.

Will they succeed? Will they live? Are rhinos nocturnal? Find out in *Tortugas Rising*, an action and adventure comedy.

**The Big Book of Dumb White Husband**

*If you're not him, you know him.*

He's challenged the grocery store. He's confronted the HOA. He's even taken on Santa himself. He doesn't usually win. These are the tales of the Dumb White Husband and they are all available here in this collected edition.

*Now you can have all the Dumb White Husband stories in one dumb place.*

**Dumb White Husband vs. the Grocery Store** - John would rather sit and watch the game, but his wife needs some things at the store. Can he complete the list and get back in time to see the end of the game?

**Dumb White Husband vs. Halloween** - Every Halloween, Chris has the scariest house on the block and gives out the best candy. But, this year, someone is showing him up and he'll stop at nothing to find out who.

**Dumb White Husband vs. Santa** - Erik has planned the perfect Christmas for his family. The plan is foolproof, bulletproof and flame retardant. Nothing can undo the hours of planning and preparation. Nothing except maybe odd-shaped packages, ill-timed fruitcakes or an errant neighborhood Santa Claus.

**Dumb White Husband vs. the Tooth Fairy** - Erik always has a plan and he's sure he would have figured out the whole Tooth Fairy thing eventually. But, when his three-year-old son takes a frisbee to the mouth, he's forced to speed things up. Between neighborhood kids with big mouths and unhelpful dentists he's going to need to improvise. Will he bend to the pressure of inflation? Will he get caught in the act? And, what do you do with those teeth anyway?

**Dumb White Husband for President (A novella)** - There comes a time in every man's life when he must stand for the things he believes in. John doesn't believe in bagging his grass. So, when a new allergy-prone neighbor gets the HOA to require it, there's only one thing he can do - run for President of The Creeks of Sage Valley Phase II.

John, Chris and Erik put aside most of their differences to run a campaign that they hope will see John elected as President and end the meddling of the rule-loving new kid on the block. Will they succeed? It's doubtful.

*Note: Previously released as Dumb White Husband for President & Other Stories*

Also, check out this guide:

**The Dumb White Husband's Guide to Babies**

Children are amazing. Their limitless capacity for love is matched only by their ability to make you feel like an idiot. Don't worry. You're not alone.

*The Dumb White Husband's Guide to Babies* tackles the subjects that other baby books ignore:

- Why you shouldn't touch the wand in the sonogram room
- The exact moment your opinion no longer counts
- How people will respond to the news

- How TV and baby classes have lied to us
- Which poop jokes to expect in the delivery room
- Converting diapers into usable guilt
- How to assure your child says your name first

*And much, much more.*

There's even a twin version in case you're so much a man that you knocked up your wife twice at the same time.

Don't go into fatherhood unprepared, read *The Dumb White Husband's Guide to Babies* today.

Visit **DumbWhiteHusband.com** and talk with other dumb white husbands. Submit your own questions to the Dumb White Husband.

**Remember this always: Together we can be dumber than any one individual can be dumb alone.**

# Giving The Bird:
# The Indie Author's Guide to Twitter

*Attention Authors:*

"Get on Twitter," they said.
"You'll sell lots of books," they said.
"They can suck it," you said.
You got on Twitter and tried to sell your books, but nothing happened. You searched for readers, but just kept attracting spam.

So, what's the point?

Twitter is a powerful marketing tool for the indie author. Within its ranks are millions of readers looking for new authors and new books. But, simply broadcasting your link isn't going to get you the attention you need.

This concise guide doesn't focus on the nuts and bolts of Twitter. It will not tell you how to gain a kabillion followers. It will tell you what "they" don't – what to tweet to build your brand as an author.

This guide is about how to sell your self as a person and a brand, one tweet at a time, to an engaged group of followers.

So, why is the guide so short? Because, just like on Twitter, it doesn't take a lot of words to communicate a powerful message.

*More about the author:*

Benjamin Wallace was born so awesome in Carleton Place, Ontario that they placed his baby picture on the front page of both town newspapers.

After that, he wrote books. This is one of those books.
He hopes you like it.

*Visit the author at benjaminwallacebooks.com*
*or dumbwhitehusband.com.*

*Also, find him on twitter @BenMWallace or on facebook.*

61123557R00125

Made in the USA
Lexington, KY
03 March 2017